DRIVEN TO KILL SERIES **BOOK 1**

DOWN THE ROAD

KATHY SIMON

Publishing Services provided by Paper Raven Books
Printed in the United States of America
First Printing, 2021

Paperback ISBN= 978-1-7373195-0-4

Casey, may you always be inspired to chase your dreams

~ CHAPTER 1 ~

A *K* AND TWO *I*'S

That red scarf blowing in the wind caught his eye as she wandered between the trucks, chatting with the drivers as they bargained with her about her fee. She was a pretty girl. Long blonde hair, bright blue eyes, but that scarf was striking. As she got closer to the truck parked in the back row of Frank's Truck Stop along Route 40 in Tennessee, he could feel that urge welling inside again. It was going to be a fun night.

Approaching the truck, she looked up through the window. "You looking for a date tonight?"

"I just might be. Why don't you come around and we can chat a bit?"

She walked to the other side of the cab, and as he opened the door, the wind caught her scarf. As it flipped over her face, the corner of his lips curled up ever so slightly. A quiet hushed chuckle slipped from his tightly closed mouth. He couldn't help himself. The Universe was waving the red cape in front of the bull, knowing that he would respond.

As she climbed into the cab and sat in the passenger's seat, she readjusted her scarf so it was under her hair. "Must be hard driving in wind this strong." She added, "My name is Kristi, with a *K* and two *I*'s."

"Nice to meet you Kristi, with a *K* and two *I*'s. They call me the Sandman, but you can call me Curtis, if you like. Either is fine."

"Well, Curtis, what did you have in mind?" A smile came upon her mouth, and her eyebrows rose with a look of deviance.

"You are a pretty girl. Why are you hanging out in truck stops? Seems like you could get higher clientele than this. Didn't your mama teach you better than that?" Curtis laughed.

"My mama? Gosh, I haven't seen my mama for five years, since I was fourteen. I'm nineteen now. Born April 15, 1974. Just had my birthday last week."

"Well then, Kristi with a *K* and two *I*'s, we should celebrate." He reached back into the sleeping berth and pulled out a bottle of red wine. "This here is a good Chilean wine. I picked it up in Asheville last time I went through there. I've been saving it for a special occasion, and this seems like the perfect reason to crack it open." He reached back in the berth again for the two glasses. "Care to reach in that glove box there and grab the corkscrew?"

"Like a Boy Scout, prepared for anything." Kristi's eyes widened as he placed the glasses on the dash and held the bottle for her to look at. "Aren't you quite the gentleman with those fancy wine glasses?"

"My mama raised a gentleman, respectful and polite, and that's what I'll always be until the end. That's a piece of her I will always have and cherish." His thoughts drifted back to a happier time. His mother would always pick up the wine bottle and read the label before it was

3

opened. It was a family ritual he had picked up over the years. He missed his mother, but a part of her lived on in him, and that gave him hope.

As he pulled open the small knife to cut the foil back, he paused for a moment, felt its weight as he rolled it in his hand. The demon emerged, and his mind took him back to the last time a "special occasion" had graced the front seat of his cab. God, it must have been two to three months. Had it really been that long? How could it be? The urge to press his fingers into a women's flesh, to caress her lips and stare into her eyes as she gasped for air.

Staring off into the darkness, remembering the last time and the times before that, he smiled.

"Are you going to open that bottle or what?" Her soft voice brought him back to the present.

"Oh, sorry." He scrambled to get the foil off and expose the cork. "I was just distracted I guess."

He twisted the corkscrew into the bottle, and finally, with a short and mighty pop, it separated from its prison of glass. Curtis poured the red liquid into the two glasses

Kristi held, filling them about halfway. Recorking the bottle, he set it in the extra-large cup holder by the driver's seat as he took a glass from Kristi.

"To you, in celebration of the day of your birth. May your days be filled with adventure and excitement, until your last moments here on earth. Cheers!"

As they raised their glasses and drank the first sip of the red wine from Chile, Curtis looked into Kristi's eyes as she gazed back.

Tilting her head slightly to the side, her eyes softened. Slight creases appeared around her eyes as the corners of her mouth turned up. Her breathing slowed and deepened. Dropping her shoulders, relaxing in his presence, she took another sip before putting her glass down. Staring at her eyes, there was something different about her. She wasn't like the others, more vested in this transaction than a typical lot lizard with a john.

"Ready to get down to business?" He glanced at the red scarf lying around her neck.

The water carried away the memory of the night before. Showering in a public restroom never got any easier. Always on guard just in case. You never know what monster may be lurking just around the corner, or maybe even hiding in plain sight. This was the life of a long-haul truck driver. A life that he chose to live. One that fit him like an old pair of boots. Boots that were well worn, the creases molded to his feet, and when he slipped his toes into them, he could feel the indentations that only years of wear could make. He felt as if he was home when he slipped them on. It was like that, this life. This was his home, his destiny.

Memories of the red scarf she wore last night filled his thoughts as he wrapped the damp towel around his neck and walked across the parking lot. As he climbed into his blue cab, he wished he had kept it. Anxious to enjoy a few days off, his foot was heavy on the throttle as he headed off for the last few hours of the drive back to the yard. Focused on the road ahead, he watched the first rays of sunshine peek out above the horizon. A sense of peace came over him. This was his favorite time of the day. It was calm and pure. The start of a new day, a new beginning.

Curtis opened his window and breathed deeply as the crisp morning air filled the cab of his truck. He loved this part of the country where the flat land gently rolled into the foothills of the Great Smoky Mountains. North Carolina and Tennessee, where tales of mystery ran deep in the mountain shadows. Tales fueled by generations of mountain folk, sitting around the campfire, sipping on their mason jars of sweet Southern nectar. Not the kind that you picked up at the local liquor store. It was the kind that you found hidden in the stump of a fallen oak just up yonder past the point of no return.

His cross-country routes from Raleigh, North Carolina, to Phoenix, Arizona, took him though this area every month. Having driven this route for the past ten years, the memories of his childhood and family whispered through his thoughts every time. The warm spring mornings, when the smell of wisteria was in the air and the new leaves were still small on the trees, those were the moments when Curtis was brought back to happier times, before the demons took over his life. Back when he and his first love, Susan, the blonde from the farm next to his, planned a future together that never came to be. They had a long history, a special bond, and he always made time to visit her when he was in town. If anyone understood why the demons came, it was Susan. They had grown up together, shared many firsts, including their first kiss. Curtis knew they were better off as friends. She would never truly accept him as a killer. She had just finished medical school and was doing her clinical residency in psychiatry. She would want to cure him and for Curtis, there was no cure.

After dropping off his rig in the lot and getting back to the farm, Curtis reached for the kitchen phone and pressed the buttons he committed to memory many years before. Soon, a familiar voice answered. Just like always.

Clearly his familiar number showed on her caller ID. "Well, howdy stranger. To what do I owe this unexpected pleasure?" A tone of sarcasm rippled through Susan's words.

"I was just thinking about you, and thought maybe you would like to grab some dinner, if you're not busy." Curtis didn't care if she was in another relationship or not. To him, it was irrelevant. The physical connection they shared would never truly disappear. He knew she couldn't resist him anymore than he could resist her.

A few hours later, Curtis pulled up in front of Susan's apartment building. As he was heading up the steps, he heard a door open. "I was just on my way up."

"I saw you pull up," Susan said as she flipped her long blonde hair. "Just thought I would save you the hassle."

"No hassle," he answered with a smile. "Shall we go?" he asked as he extended his hand.

As she took his hand, she rolled her eyes.

"You are too independent for your own good, my friend."

Susan and Curtis pulled up to a neighborhood Chinese restaurant and sat down in a booth.

Curtis reached into his pocket and pulled out some coins, a nickel, three pennies, two quarters, and a dime. He turned over the paper placemat in front of him showing the Chinese zodiac. Thankfully, the other side was blank. He placed the coins on the white field and smiled as he looked across the table at Susan.

"I have a new game." He motioned to the coins randomly scattered on the piece of paper. "Describe to me what you see."

"What are you talking about, Curtis?" Annoyance lit her voice. "Why do you always want to play mind games?"

"This isn't a mind game. It's a tool to understand how people process information so that you can improve the communication in your relationships." He leaned back, content with his response. He was pretty proud that he pulled that one out of his ass, and it sounded pretty believable too.

Eyeing him with a cautious look, she pursed her lips. "But we aren't in a relationship anymore."

"Not a committed, monogamous one, but we do have a relationship," he said as the waitress approached to take their order. After ordering, Curtis returned to their previous conversation. "Just play along."

"Fine. I see coins on a piece of paper. I also see an ass before me that isn't going to get any from me and won't be able to buy any with only sixty-eight cents in his pocket." She laughed at the sneer that moved across Curtis's face.

"Is that all, really all, you see? Come on."

He knew this game all too well. She said that all the time, "none for you," but once he moved to kiss her good night, she just couldn't resist him.

"Okay. I see three copper coins. I see four silver coins. Three pennies, two quarters, one dime, and one nickel."

"Anything else?" Curtis prodded once again.

"No, nothing else. Just a bunch of coins on a page. Final answer!" She snickered. "So what does that tell you about my inner psyche?"

"Well, it tells me you are a 'same person.' You look for similarities in things. You gain confidence in doing new things and taking on new challenges when you can relate them to things you have achieved that are similar. You notice differences, but as a mechanism to bring them back together again. You focus on the big picture first then dive into the details to understand the main point, the take-home message. You want to be in charge; you are a visionary leader, that really wants to eat some Chinese food and have your way with me later, just like old times."

The waitress approached carrying their plates.

Susan shook her head as she closed her eyes letting out a puff of air. "Here's our food. Perfect timing," she said, obviously welcoming the interruption to end that topic of conversation.

As the waitress walked away, Susan asked, "How are Pappy and Grandma doing? I miss seeing them. Lots of great memories driving to the Tennessee mountains and hanging out around the campfire." She poured the soy sauce over her fried rice.

"They are doing well. It's been almost ten years since Mama died, but we all have figured out how to live without her."

"Your mother was a wonderful woman and left way too early. I wish none of us ever experienced that. But I'm glad Pappy and Grandma are doing well."

"I know they miss you. Pappy still tells stories around the campfire, tinkers in the workshop, and Grandma bakes tasty treats for anyone who stops by."

"Good times. I loved the smell of fresh baked cookies that greeted you as soon as you entered the door."

"When the door and windows were open, the fan blew the smell onto the front porch," he added as he ate the last bite of his meal. "I would be fifty pounds more if I lived with them. I can't resist Grandma's cookies. They are blue-ribbon worthy, no doubt."

"You still look good despite all the cookies you've devoured over the years." A twinkle shown in her eyes, and a smile crept across her lips.

The conversation drifted to Susan's residency. "I am focusing on antisocial personality disorders."

"Must have been all those long talks about serial killers while we were growing up." Curtis laughed as he said it.

"How is everything?" The waitress said as she returned to check on them.

"Everything is great," Curtis replied.

As she walked away, Curtis couldn't help but wonder what her story was. Her heavily wrinkled face showed the years of stress that she had endured. "So have you figured out the trigger that made someone snap and start killing? Or were they just born killers?"

"I can't talk about my cases. I still think there is an incident that causes them to believe what they are doing is justified. Perhaps a loss that makes them believe things can't go on the way they always have. They can no longer hide their demons."

Curtis stared at Susan. *Was she reading my mind?*

"Maybe," was all he said.

"Can I get you anything else?" the waitress asked as she picked up their empty plates, interrupting their moment.

"No, thank you. It was perfect!" Curtis said as their eyes met. "Thank you so much for serving us a most wonderful meal."

"Glad you enjoyed it. Here's your check. No rush, please stay as long as you like."

He could tell Susan was getting annoyed. He quickly responded, "Oh, here you go." He picked up the brown leather folio, glanced at the total, and pulled the bills from his wallet and placed them in the leather book. As he snapped it shut with a firm click, he added, "We're good. Thanks again!"

As she reached for the worn leather book, he smiled and held it for a bit too long, allowing his hand to momentarily meet hers.

They both noticed the involuntary twitch as it passed through her body when their hands met, and her eyes fixed on his face.

"Thank you. And please come back and see us again." A blush crept across her face.

"Oh, we will see you again. This is becoming our favorite Chinese restaurant, and you are definitely our favorite server!" Curtis returned her gaze with a little raise of his eyebrows.

Susan's eyes narrowed, and she glanced between the blushing waitress and Curtis. "Thank you again," Susan said, the annoyance in her voice evident to all.

Glaring at Susan, the waitress added with a smile, "Oh yes, you both are most welcome." She turned her head towards Curtis and held his stare for what he knew was a little too long for Susan's comfort.

Curtis returned his attention back to Susan as she grunted and shook her head in disbelief. Curtis knew his energy attracted people. He was surprised that Susan's jealous streak was so evident. They hadn't been in a committed relationship since she went off to college the summer after his mother's death.

"Let's get out of here." He reached across the table and gently stroked Susan's hand. "After you." He motioned to her. *Always the gentleman, Curtis.* The voice of his mother echoed in his ears. One thing for certain, she had made sure that his manners were impeccable.

As they made their way to the restaurant door, Curtis glanced over his shoulder one last time. As he reached for the door, he took note that the older waitress was smiling sweetly as she watched him leave. He gave her one last nod as he raised his eyebrows, as if to say "until next time." Her smile grew larger as she turned away, the red tone crept across her face once again.

Curtis would see her again. He would protect her and save her from her continued life of loneliness, comforted by meaningless interactions with strangers as she served them food. She was attractive for an older woman; obviously she would be attracted to him. He was sure that given his attention, she would do anything he asked, willingly.

He'd bet she had a scarf somewhere in her closet. Staring off into space, he touched his neck and began to mindlessly stroke the space under his Adam's apple. Just needed to figure out the timing, he mused. His hand stopped as he noticed what he was doing.

This one would be his next rendezvous. The details would be easy; details were always easy. He loved the planning. As he came back to the present—and Susan— he blinked as if waking.

He could feel the passion flying between them as they reached the car. Walking to the passenger side, he opened the door and watched her slide onto the soft leather of the Mustang's seat. He shut the door and jogged around to the driver's side and quickly jumped in behind the black-leather steering wheel. Glancing over at Susan, their eyes met, and he gave her his infamous eyebrow nod. They both laughed out loud. Susan leaned in and their lips met. Curtis could feel the hardness growing in his jeans, the chemistry between them was palatable.

"Let's get out of here." Susan fell back into her seat, breathless just from the kiss.

"Absolutely, babe! You read my mind." He turned the key, and the engine roared to life. As he found reverse on the shifter and laid his arm over her seat, he looked over his shoulder and backed up out of the parking spot.

~ CHAPTER 2 ~

THE WAITRESS

Curtis had a few days before his next trip, so he decided to head to the beach to collect his thoughts and plan his next outing. Sitting on the beach, he watched the sky grow darker as the sun set behind him. In the darkness, Curtis listened to the crash of the waves roaring like a freight train or a thunderstorm. Listening carefully, he could hear the waves gather momentum before they erupted with a loud thunderous crash smashing into the sand.

The ocean always reminded Curtis of the demon within him. The uncaged raw energy of the surf, the vast horizon that went on forever, the inability to be controlled. Similar to how the shore yearned to not be revenged by the pounding surf, Curtis wished to control his urge to kill. But alas, as the ocean makes its mark on the sand, Curtis made his mark on society. They both changed the environment around them, a new destiny continually carved out of the sand. Metamorphosed into a new landscape. No trace left behind of what existed, the ultimate chameleon. The one force that cannot be tamed.

The seagulls heckled, unsettled, as they scanned the shoreline for their next meal, the next victim. The sound brought to mind Curtis's next victim. He saw her face, that shy smile. Her eyes danced, hypnotized by his. He had watched her for several months secretly even before the dinner with Susan at the Chinese restaurant. She was older, yes, but she still had passion. He knew that he could unleash her carnal lust for a man. He was at least twenty years her junior. He was barely twenty-eight; she was in her early-to-mid fifties. The wrinkles around her eyes, between her breasts, and the spots on her hands told of the struggles she had endured. Scars on her arms told him that people were not always kind to her. He knew what he needed to be done. He spent the night in the hotel overlooking the beach, the balcony door open, the sound of the crashing waves filled the hotel room. Curtis slept more soundly than he had in a while. His conscience was clear, his path determined. It was the calm before the storm.

The next morning Curtis headed home and spent the afternoon at his farm. As the sun started setting, he jumped in his red Mustang and headed out. The moon was still rising as he pulled into the Chinese restaurant lot and maneuvered his car to the back where the employees parked. She was almost to her car when a familiar voice called out, "Hi, pretty lady. You certainly do look beautiful in the moonlight." Curtis caught the smile on her face as she turned around.

Curtis noticed the moonlight as it sparkled in her eyes. "Well, fancy seeing you here," she joked in a flirty way. "To what do I owe this unexpected pleasure?"

"I know you might not believe me, but I just can't stop thinking about you," Curtis said, matching her coyness tone for tone.

"Really? Well truth be told, you have entered my thoughts a time or two as well." She ran her tongue across her lips.

He walked closer to her. "I'm happy to hear that."

As she reached her car, instead of getting in, she leaned against the door. "Well, this is me."

Not missing a beat to lure in his prey, Curtis joined her and rested next to her against the car. Less confrontational to stand side by side. His every move was calculated, every word practiced. The game of cat and mouse was always the focus for Curtis. He wanted them to submit, to welcome his control as his prey became a willing partner. He had a demonic side, but he was not a monster; he only did what they wanted, what they needed him to do.

"I'm sure you're tired and had a long day, but I thought

maybe we could take a ride and just talk." He lowered his head to avoid eye contact as he prepared himself for the ultimate rejection, so it appeared.

"Well, why not," she replied.

He lifted his head, and their eyes met. A large smile grew across his face. "Okay then, let's go!"

He extended his hand, and she eagerly took it, and they headed off towards his Mustang. He opened the car door for her, and she graciously moved in close to him. They were intimately close. His breath was on her neck. She let out a quiet sigh and turned to look up at him, slid her hand up behind his neck, raised her chin, and parted her lips.

Yes, this will be so easy. Curtis bent to meet her yearning lips. Her knees buckled as she fell against his chest. This was going to be an awesome night. His arms caught her and held her.

After driving for over an hour out into the countryside, Curtis turned into a long driveway that headed between pastures full of cows.

"Can we go down here?" she asked.

"Yeah, we are fine here. I know the owner." He gave her his sultry eyebrow wink.

She giggled like a schoolgirl. They pulled off behind the barn, and Curtis turned off the Mustang. Looking over at his lady, Curtis inquired, "Want to take a look around?"

"Absolutely!"

They walked towards the barn, and she reached out and took his hand. He looked at her and smiled. Good thing he brought the scarf he kept in the glove compartment in his car.

As they reached the barn and headed inside, there was a line of hay bales set up along one side with a cooler. Curtis led her over to the makeshift seating area and leaned behind the bales and pulled out a blanket. "Let's sit on this. The hay can be scratchy."

"Such a gentleman. I find that so attractive. Most young people don't think like that anymore. You are different."

"I am different in many ways."

She moved closer to him and rested her head on his shoulder. "I haven't known you for very long, but I do know you make me feel safe."

Curtis wrapped his arm around her shoulder as his other hand gently touched her chin as he turned her face towards his. "I couldn't help but notice the scars on your arms. You wear them proudly, as you should. I want you to know that I would never inflict harm on a woman like that."

She smiled broadly, "Thank you for that. Those are from a long time ago. But the marks are a constant reminder of what I went through, and that I will never forget. It was from a man that was not kind, unlike you. Although I thought he loved me, I was mistaken, as true love doesn't do this." She pointed to the scars from cuts and burns on her arms. "There are many more scars that you cannot see, as well."

"I'm sorry he did that to you. You deserve to be honored and held in highest esteem." He cupped her face in both his hands. "You didn't deserve that."

Curtis paused a second before he gently kissed her lips.

She closed her eyes and passionately pressed against his body as they continued. As she laid her head on his shoulder and looked down, she noticed a piece of fabric sticking out of the pocket in his jeans. "What's that in your pocket?"

He laughed and pulled the fabric out of its secret hiding place. "That is a scarf I brought with me." He gauged her reaction on her face and continued. "I thought you may want to tie back your hair if we put the top down on the Mustang."

The smile on her face grew big as she cupped his face in her hands and kissed him. "You are one of a kind! But maybe we can find another use for that scarf," she mused.

"Just what do you have in mind, my lady?" Curtis flapped the scarf in the air and twisted it around his wrists.

She reached for the scarf. "I like the element of surprise." She placed the scarf over her eyes and knotted it behind her head. Her lips parted, her chest rose and fell as her breath quickened, and he turned towards her.

His mouth met hers with anticipation of what was to come. *She would never be hurt again.* He noticed her bare neck, its delicate structure as his fingers gently caressed from behind her ear down to her collarbone. His touch was met with a gasp as she trembled. He kissed her as he unbuttoned her blouse and dropped it to the ground. He felt her shiver each time he touched her.

"You are a beautiful woman, and I promise I won't let anyone hurt you again." He kissed her and brought his hands to her neck. He pressed his fingers into the side of her throat as his thumb dug in on the opposite side.

"Not so hard," her voice cracked as his hands pressed harder on her throat. She strained, arms extended trying to push him away.

He pulled back from her with his head slightly tilted so he could see her face; his hands never left her throat.

She gasped, trying to get air into her lungs as his vise-like grip started crushing her airway. He removed one hand from her throat, tugged the blindfold off, and swiftly replaced it on her neck. She blinked, stared at his face, as her eyes filled with terror as she saw the monster that was in front of her.

Curtis looked into her eyes. The veins in his arms bulged under the strain of his muscles. He wanted to be the last thing she saw as she took her last breath.

She gasped one final time. He dug his fingers into her flesh, and she started to shake. Pressing all his body weight against her, she struggled, and her eyes started bulging ever so slightly, until there was nothing but silence. Her muscles became limp.

His chest puffed up as he admired his work. Another woman saved from the pain and heartache of unhealthy relationships. He held her arm and shook his head as he looked over each scar; she would never again be exposed to the pain that caused those. He organized her things and headed over to the adjacent outbuilding that housed the old meat grinder. He was grateful to still have the family cattle farm. He no longer was involved in the daily running of the business, but still living on the property certainly had its perks.

The overhead light flicked as the electricity started to flow before glowing steadily in the night. This grinder was formerly used to dispose of deceased cattle, and now Curtis often used it to dispose of other carcasses. The chute was too small, so he dismembered her as the motor roared to life. He mixed the minced flesh with some feed and headed out to put it in the feeding troughs. "Bon appétit!" he said as a few of the cattle made their way over. He headed back to the grinder, cleaned it up, and gathered up everything from the barn, and headed out to his car. He wrapped the scarf around his neck as he got into the Mustang.

Curtis made the familiar turn through the stone gate onto the winding drive up to the plantation house. The window was down so he could drink in the cool night air. "I could really use a drink." He parked and walked up the steps to the front door. Taking one final look at the moon high in the sky, he looked at his watch. 2:20 a.m.

He shook his head.

He walked quietly into the kitchen as if trying not to disturb anyone. Even though Curtis lived alone, he still acted as if it was his mother's home. He opened the fridge, grabbed the pitcher of sweet tea and, grabbing a glass from the cabinet, poured himself a glass and headed upstairs to shower and go to bed. As his head hit his pillow, a smile crept onto his lips, and he could hear his mother's voice in his head, "Sleep well, my sweet boy!"

~ CHAPTER 3 ~

THE FAMILY BUSINESS

Ten years before on a warm spring day, Curtis had returned home earlier than expected after spending the weekend with Susan down at the beach with her family. They were both seniors in high school and only a few months shy of graduation. He had made good time as he looked at his watch, and it read 2:20 p.m. as he headed up the stairs.

The house was eerily quiet. He noticed his parents' door was closed, which was unusual this time of day. Something drew him down the hall, and he knocked softly on the door. He waited silently; there was no response. Laying his hand on the knob, slowly he turned it, placing his other hand on the door in an attempt to muffle any potential sound. Peeking around the edge of the door, Curtis whispered, "Mom, are you asleep?"

As he looked around the room, he caught a strong odor of her favorite incense coming from the bathroom. Looking that direction, he said in a loud voice, "Hey Mom, I'm home. Got home a bit early." His call was met with deafening silence. He sensed something was wrong and took a few steps towards the open bathroom door when he saw her lying in the tub colored crimson with her blood.

The next few hours, Curtis sat in disbelief as police, paramedics, and his father arrived. How could his mom be gone? How could she have taken her own life and left him? The demons within him began to grow restless. He had never felt such rage before.

She was such a selfish bitch, he thought to himself.

As he looked around the room, he saw his father sitting at the kitchen table, his hands restless as he played with his drink. *It was his fault! He caused this! If it wasn't for his father and his stupid mistress, Mama would still be here! He should be the one whose blood is spilled. He needs to pay! Him and that bitch!*

His thoughts scared him as he stood there staring at his father. What was wrong with him? What kind of monster was he? His mom sensed when he struggled to keep them at bay and would stay by his side, giving him the strength to control his anger and urges. She was gone. The anger boiled inside him like nothing he had ever experienced before. He knew who was responsible for his mom's unbearable pain; pain so great she chose to end her life rather than continue. Curtis would harness the power of the demon within him and avenge her death.

The next few weeks were a blur. The funeral was delayed due to the medical examiner having to certify her death as a suicide, hours of interviews, and endless questions. Curtis had told the story so many times. Susan was by his side throughout it all. Holding him up when he wasn't able to stand, offering a shoulder for him to cry on, listening while he screamed in rage.

After Mama's funeral, Curtis decided to spend some time in Tennessee with Pappy and Grandma. Dad stayed behind to take care of affairs at the farm and had appointments with the attorneys set up for the next week to start the necessary modifications for the estate and businesses. Pappy and Grandma had already headed back to their home. Susan decided to hang back as well, so it was just Curtis. As he put his bag in the back of the Mustang, he thought this would be a good time to come clean with Grandpappy. When he turned the key, the engine roared to life. He pushed on the gas and drove down the drive and through the stone gate like so many times before. But this wasn't like any other trip.

This would be the trip where he would finally be able to understand what coursed through his veins, its history, figure out where it came from, and how could he contain it.

Growing up south of the Mason-Dixon line, essential oil, or moonshine to the commoners, was a rite of passage for everyone. Even as a child, when he would visit Grandpappy's house in eastern Tennessee, there normally was a big blue barrel full of mash fermenting in the basement, and the old copper still was tucked away in the shed. When he was a teenager, Grandpappy would let him sneak out to the shed at night as they set up the still. He learned early how to collect the heads, hearts, and tails as the alcohol came out of the still. He taught him how to cut the distillate just right to get the best flavor.

Curtis remembered growing up. Pappy and his friends hanging out at the house drinking from their mason jars around the fire. They were always tinkering with something—a car, a tractor, a truck—planning their next brew, and in recent years, talking about the good ole days. Curtis's mother always loved going to her father's house. It was a place that she got energy from, felt rejuvenated, and could recharge her battery. Curtis felt the same way. He always connected with Grandpappy in a special way.

During high school, Curtis and Susan would drive

out to Pappy's for long weekends during the summer. Fueled by their imagination, they would be deep in conversation about what drove various serial killers and mass murderers. Sometimes those conversations would spill over to their fireside chats. Grandpappy always seemed a little too interested. Often seeming to have firsthand knowledge to add to the discussion. There had been more than a couple of instances when he described things a little too realistically.

Susan questioned him saying, "Seems like you are speaking from personal experience there, Pappy?"

Pappy would respond with his typical smirk, leaning back in his chair. "Well, when you've lived as long as I, you've seen a lot of things."

And that was always the clue to move on, but one day, Curtis knew he was going to ask him. Maybe this trip Curtis would find the courage to ask the burning question.

Six hours later, the Mustang pulled into the Mason homestead. Pappy and Grandma would hear him coming down the drive, and he was sure that good old

Tucker would give out his warning howl alerting them of imminent visitors. As he parked in front of the house, the front door opened, and that brown hound dog bounded down the steps.

"You made good time, boy. Guess there wasn't much traffic?" Pappy said as Grandma made her way down the steps arms outstretched as she rushed to give Curtis a hug.

"Just buzzed right through. No issues at all."

"Curtis, come inside. I'm sure you are starving. Darryl, get his bag for him, and Tucker, come on," Grandma commanded. Just like Mom, Grandma ruled the roost. People just naturally obeyed and rarely questioned her orders. She had a calm presence about her. Her silver-and-white hair was always pinned up on her head. Only at formal events did she wear it down. "It gets in my way," she always said. They all followed her inside and gathered at the kitchen table. Grandma pulled out a big bowl of her famous pork barbecue. Spending time with family around the table, this was the part of his life with his mother that he would miss most.

After they were done, Grandma said, "Pappy, why don't you and Curtis head out to the shed. I'm sure there is something you can find to tinker with."

Without hesitation, Pappy and Curtis pushed their chairs back, collected their plates, placed them in the sink, and headed out the back door. The old wooden screen door slammed shut on the 1932 farmhouse with a thunderous crack that always reminded Curtis of the country and tradition. It was often a game he and his cousin would play, trying to see how many of them could scurry through the door before it would slam shut. It was fun until someone got smacked with the door in the face as they weren't quite quick enough.

They made their way to the shed. Pappy put his arm around Curtis's shoulder. "Curtis, it means a lot to your grandma and me that you are here with us during this time. It was hard seeing your mother laid to rest. The ceremony was beautiful and fitting for the princess that she was, but we all would rather have that angel here with us." There was nothing to add. Pappy was right. Mom belonged with them.

As they neared the shed, Curtis caught a whiff of that familiar sweet smell. Something was brewing in those big blue mash barrels. "What oils are you making?"

"Oh, you have your mother's nose, don't you son? I'm trying something new. Something to honor your mama. Not sure how it's going to turn out, but it should be a special flowery brandy of lavender and berries. I thought it would capture her personality well."

"I think she would be very honored, I really do. Will you let me try some? You know I am almost eighteen."

"With everything you've been through in the past weeks, it's only fitting that you get the first taste of Deb's Mountain Oil."

Not that he hadn't snuck a jar or two of the family brew, but this would be the first time he would openly taste the sweet smooth liquor that came from that old copper still in the shed. "It's almost time to move to the distillation step. I think my ole buddy Floyd was planning on swinging up this way over the weekend. Perhaps you would like to help us?"

"Absolutely! I would love that."

When the weekend came, Curtis, Pappy, and Floyd headed out to the old shed right after breakfast. They worked all day, running the still and bottling up their mountain gold in the mason jars that Grandma had brought out. "Clean and sanitized for your protection!" She left the trays of pint ball jars and lids on the worktable in the shed. "You boys need anything else?"

"No, honey, we are all set. Should have the first tasting ready after supper," Pappy responded.

As they all gathered around the firepit after dinner, Floyd went over and grabbed a pint jar from the shed. They poured a bit in four glasses, and Pappy held up his glass. "To our beautiful Debra. May this spirit honor you and help bring us peace as we find a new way to live without you here with us in this world."

They all took a sip, and Floyd said, "Oh, that's nice. It's going to mellow nicely in the cherry barrels too. Should give it a nice deep color." They all agreed that it was a fine spirit, worthy of his mother's memory and name. Deb's Mountain Oil was born. Curtis was quite pleased with his newfound talent as a mountain chemist.

As the evening rolled on, Grandma went inside to work on her crossword puzzles. She loved those things. And Floyd bid his farewell. Pappy said, "And then there were two."

Looking at the fire, mesmerized by the dancing flame, Curtis's thoughts began to wander back to the last time he and Susan were here and Pappy seemed to be hiding a secret. Was now the right time? How could he know? How would Pappy react? What if his gut was wrong? What if it was only him that thought this way? What if it wasn't "in his blood" after all? He would never know unless he asked.

He mustered up the courage to speak. "Pappy? Do you think people deserve to die?"

Pappy took a sip of whiskey, cleared his throat, and began to speak in a very hushed, almost reverent tone. "Curtis, there are times in life when one must atone for their sins. Sometimes this is taken care of naturally, but other times it's not." He studied Curtis. Grandpappy was clearly gauging whether he should continue.

Curtis's eyes were wide as he leaned forward and rested his forearms on his thighs. "Exactly." He silently urged Pappy to go on.

"Sometimes order and balance need a little help to be restored. The Bible teaches us 'an eye for an eye.' The rules of civilized society can be at odds with what is just and right, what is required to maintain balance. Sometimes, a man must make order out of chaos. But he also must control the urge to unleash the demons too early." Pappy took a long sip of the mellow whiskey, his daughter's whiskey, her story. His last words lingered long in the cool night air.

Demons? Why did he use those words? Did he know about the demons? Did Mama tell him?

After what seemed like an eternity, the stillness of the night was punctuated by the rhythmic calls of the barred owl. *Hoo*, HOO, *hoo*, *hoo*. Again and again, the sound drilled into his head. Curtis broke the silence. "Pappy, do you think one is called to restore order?"

Pappy took another sip of the calming elixir. "Curtis, I believe that we all have a divine purpose, a gift that we are destined to share with the world. This gift will allow us to leave our mark, etch the fact that we not only existed in this life, we thrived. For some, this mark is shallow and barely noticeable; for others, it cuts deep. It scars many and even harms some. These deep marks are the ones that truly change the course of the Universe. Like a river carves a path in stone, some people carve a path through humanity. They are true warriors. They are key enablers to maintaining order in our civilized society. They are the keepers of justice, the ones that levy penance and drive accountability. You, son, come from a long line of these heroes and heroines. My grandpappy and I are heroes, and I believe it runs through you as well." Lowering his head, Pappy swirled his glass, the ice cubes clanking against the sides as the owl continued its call for a mate.

"Pappy, it does run through me, the Mason lifeblood.

The demons often torment me. I don't know how long I can keep them at bay. Mom helped me. She would sense when they were near."

"She had a special gift. She saw beyond the natural world." The ice in Pappy's glass clinked as he sipped.

"She would often come through the house with burning sage. The smell still is a comfort."

Pappy smiled and nodded.

"I don't know what I will do without her. How will I stop it? The rage? The urge?"

"Curtis, some day you will find someone to help you. When the time is right, you will know. Remember, fate will intervene, and you will do what needs to be done."

"I will continue to make you proud and bring honor to our family and to Mom's memory."

Pappy raised his glass towards him and added in his typical jovial manner, "Welcome to the family business, Curtis." They both laughed as their glasses met.

Curtis felt not only relief but belonging as he sat enjoying this moment beside his grandfather, his lifeblood. At last, he had someone who understood. Who shared his secret in a way few did. To many they were killers, but to each other they were warriors. The ones that cleansed the vile filth and sewage from the bowels of humanity. They were the keepers of civilization. They were the heroes and heroines, as Pappy said. Curtis felt a sense of pride. His name may be MacIntyre, but he was a Mason through and through.

Curtis struggled with what needed to come next. How to confide in Grandpappy. How would he tell him that he had crossed the line, that the demons had won? He felt justified in doing it. Like Pappy said, sometimes you need to deliver justice yourself. Maybe it was the guilt mixed with the liquor, but Curtis decided to jump in with both feet. "Pappy, I have to tell you. I delivered justice for Mom. It needed to be done."

"What happened?"

"He kept saying that she would come back. She won't raise the baby on her own. Pappy, I knew of my father's affair for a long time, but I never said anything.

I came home early from a friend's house and found Dad and Candice in bed. I didn't tell Mom and believed Dad would break it off like the others, but he didn't. He knocked her up. You know Mom couldn't take that kind of humiliation. She was a proud woman and prided herself on maintaining a high moral standard, and her family needed to as well. What would people think? She couldn't take that. Candice didn't care. Her actions caused Mom to end her life." He lowered his head and paused as he regained his composure.

He looked straight into Pappy eyes. "I did what I had to do, what you would have done. I sought justice for Mom." His fist clenched as he spoke. "Mom couldn't do it for herself, so I did. I tracked Candice down, seduced her into coming with me to the fields, and used the blue scarf she was wearing, tied her up, and slowly started suffocating her with the scarf. As she struggled, I looked straight into her eyes. I never broke eye contact. I saw when she realized that her time was limited, that she would die, and that I would be the reason." He stared at

Pappy as he searched for some sign.

"I suspected you had something to do with her disappearance."

"You don't seem surprised?"

"I'm not." A gleam of pride drifted across his face.

"I have never felt anything as exhilarating as this before. The more she struggled, the more I realized that it was different, this was something more powerful, more sinister." The excitement welled within him as he retold the story. "I was hunting my prey just like a lion that latches onto the neck of the antelope and bites harder, deeper as the animal continues to struggle. The more it struggles, the tighter the grip. As Candice continued to struggle, I dropped the scarf and gripped her neck with both my hands, pressed my fingers into her flesh. I felt her trachea crushing under my powerful hands."

He acted out the kill, sitting on the edge of his seat, pretending his hands were wrapped around her throat like that very day. "Hands of an athlete. I never realized how strong I was. I was able to squeeze the life out of someone. Someone who deserved to die. Someone I needed to remove to cure my guilt to seek justice for Mom, to save other women from the pain that Mom endured from this whore. As the bitch lay motionless on the ground, I loosened my grip ever so slightly. I looked down at her eyes, realized that there was nothing left. She would no longer haunt us. Mom would finally be able to rest comfortably. I had accomplished my mission, I had triumphed over evil."

He lowered his hands as if he were removing them from her neck. She was his first kill, and he had enjoyed it. He puffed out his chest as he looked down at his hands. He was the mighty hunter, the lion, king of the jungle. He looked up to meet Pappy's gaze. He searched Pappy's face for some sign, some signal that he had done the right thing.

Pappy sat motionless for what seemed like hours. Finally, he spoke. "Curtis, what did you do with the body?"

"I put her in the trunk of the Mustang and took her

back to the farm. I used the meat grinder in the old shed." Good thing the barn had the grinder to mince meat for the cows. It was an old technique that was no longer used since mad cow disease cropped up, but the grinder was still in the feed shed, and it made for the perfect way to dispose of the evidence. "I was very thorough in the cleanup. I disinfected everything and took it all apart to clean every nook and cranny, Pappy. There isn't a trace anywhere."

"That's good, son. I think you did good for your first time. But there are a lot of cops snooping around, and your Dad, you, and I are prime suspects, as you know. We need to play the grieving family, and we need to distance ourselves from your dad. To protect you, we need to keep him at arm's length. A Mason always has a plan and a backup plan or two."

Curtis was relieved. He knew his Pappy would protect him. "Thank you, Pappy. It won't be hard to stay away from Dad; he is just as much to blame."

"Don't go getting any ideas, Curtis. Your father needs

to stay alive and not disappear, at least for now. You have done your part. You let me handle your father. You just promise me you will never forgive him or Candice for taking Deb from us."

"Oh, you don't have to worry. That will never happen. They will pay for what they did. Actually, one already has," he added with a bit of an egotistical sneer.

"Well played, son. Well played."

~ CHAPTER 4 ~

THE THREAD

From her office above Michigan Avenue overlooking the Chicago River on the fifth floor of the *Chicago Tribune* building, Kaylee Smith-Roberts sifted through files of news articles dated over the past five years. There was a series of crimes along a route across the southern US from coast to coast, North Carolina to California. Kaylee didn't believe in random chance. Things just didn't happen by chance; there was no random. And she had a sixth sense when it came to the dark side. Her scientific nature drove her to continue to question, to ask *why* well beyond that which would drive most people crazy.

With the articles scattered on the long, wooden table, she pushed them around, reorganized them, searching for a common thread. "What is hiding in plain sight? Come on, Kaylee, read between the lines, break the code," she mused. Her method involved moving from topic to topic, dabbling here and there, dipping her toe in to test the waters, able to move on to another pool. This controlled chaos, as she termed it, was how she processed information. It wasn't linear, it wasn't in any specific order. It was free form, chaotic to most, fearful to some, and frustrating for all who knew her.

One day she hoped she would be able to find the Clyde to her Bonnie. Her partner in crime. That other person that would finally "get" her. Be able to spar with her, take her personal jabs in stride, take pleasure in a little pain, be willing to walk on the dark side with her. Did this person exist? In her dreams he did. Maybe one day, when she least expected it, he would reveal himself to her and her destiny would be visible. But until then, she was content to search the data of unsolved cases for clues, for patterns that only she believed existed.

As her green eyes darted across the information, scanning, ever scanning for clues that would make themselves visible at the right time, something caught her attention. An unsolved crime of a single lady in a small North Carolina town. Just outside Raleigh. A woman disappeared in the spring of 1983, and not a sign of her was ever found again. It had been over ten years. Kaylee picked up the folder containing the article. Its weight felt heavy on her heart. Quickly scanning the article and thumbing through the copies of the police report, Kaylee came upon the pictures of the missing woman. A beautiful, blonde girl. Candice Jordan, 28, Chapel Hill, North Carolina. Last whereabouts was her work.

"Interviews with her work colleagues suggest she had plans to spend the weekend out of town. She was reported missing on Monday afternoon when she didn't show up at work and no one could reach her." Speaking helped Kaylee use several senses to process information more quickly. Her constant talking to herself often drove her coworkers crazy, which was why she had always been assigned a private office. There were some perks to her batshit crazy behaviors.

"What is it about Candice that intrigues me?" She studied the picture of the young woman. Blue eyes, blonde hair. In the picture she was wearing a designer scarf. Not many women wore scarves anymore. Why was she? It was a long, thin scarf. One that could be used as a blindfold. Why did she wear it to work that day? The picture was from the security camera as she exited the building for the day. She was dressed fairly casually, in jeans and a blouse, had sandals on and this scarf. Maybe she drove a convertible, or her date did, and she needed it to tie her hair. Maybe she used it to tie something else or someone else, or maybe herself.

"Kay, where are you going with this?" She laughed out loud. "Perhaps it's time to call it a night." Kaylee looked down at her gold watch she had picked up at a jeweler on Fifth Avenue in New York City. She always wore a watch.

For some reason, Kaylee just couldn't let go of the scarf. Not sure what it was that drew her to it, but she knew that her gut was rarely wrong. Not only did she have a background in journalism, she had a criminology degree, and chasing down unsolved crimes was just up her alley. She'd go toe-to-toe with any watchdog reporter, detective, or even the experts at the Bureau's Behavioral Analysis Unit.

She walked back to the table and opened all the folders, moving the missing women's pictures to the top of each pile. Picture by picture, she expertly scanned for clues, for differences, for similarities. She was a "same" person, and her research had taught her that most serial killers were "same" people too. Sometimes the similarities were obvious; sometimes they were much more subtle. Many times an outsider could never figure out the thread that tied them all together.

But the psyche of the killer drove them to always have a thread. Often it was the trigger that caused them to kill in the first place. Often it became their trophy, the little piece that reminded them of their mission. It allowed them to relive that experience, that high that they got from it all. The satisfaction, the revenge, the justice. Many psychotherapists said that serial killers couldn't feel empathy, that they couldn't feel anything.

"They feel. They feel differently than most, but feel they do. They experience emotion in a more vibrant way. They see things in spectrums of color, not just the normal rainbow." Kaylee knew this, because she saw things differently as well. She believed the Universe sent her subtle clues. She followed the breadcrumbs left unnoticed by most, even the best detectives and the FBI's top profilers. They had nothing on Kaylee Smith-Roberts.

The world saw a confident, independent, and powerful woman. That was the persona she emitted to the outside world. Kaylee rarely let anyone close to her; she kept most people at arm's length. This was the coping measure she had perfected as a small child. She carried the burden of horrible abuse at the hands of her stepfather. She finally overcame him one night, smashing his skull with a candlestick she had hidden under her pillow. It was fifteen years ago, when she was only thirteen, but the memory was etched in her psyche so vividly she would never forget.

What scared her more than the monster that she fought that night was the way that she felt while she was doing it. As the blood spattered her face each time she lifted the candlestick, it gave her more power. The sound of his skull breaking made her clench her teeth harder to drive the object deeper into his brain. The fact that Kaylee enjoyed, rejoiced in this violence scared her more than anything. Could she really be a killer at her innermost core? "No, I help the victims. I am one of the good guys." She refocused on the clues.

As she looked at the picture, she saw some victims with scarfs, but most not. The pictures of the bodies showed women of various complexions, hair colors. The age span was rather large as well, nineteen to fifty-three. Most killers focused on specific types.

But there must be a clue; somewhere, in these pictures, was a clue, Kaylee knew it.

Frustrated, she made a note of the scarf and moved on to focus on the locations of the body dumps. All along major interstates and highways. These roads were heavily traveled for the most part. Just by looking, the dates and locations didn't seem to follow any set pattern, but there was always a pattern. Kaylee decided to plot the dates and locations on a map and see what popped up.

"Bingo!" she yelled. "This is it!" She stood back and admired her newly found link. "All of the kills line up perfectly on a consistent route from LA to Norfolk, Virginia. Could it be a long-haul truck driver? They drive the same routes again and again. They are loners, working solo for the most part."

She ran her fingers through her long, dark hair. It felt soft, silky. As she twirled her hair, the scent of her shampoo entered her nose. Maybe she was onto something. She'd continue this research another day. It was late, and she needed a beer. She saved the maps and left a note for her assistant to print it and have it on her table in the morning. Switching off her computer, she turned to go. Smiling smugly at her reflection in the window, she was happy with her progress today. Leaving the files on the table, she walked over and flipped off the light, exited her office, and headed to the elevators.

The morning sun was just starting to peek into her window and shine on the papers she left scattered the night before as Kaylee opened her office door. Her blinds were always at the top of her window. She enjoyed watching the world go by as she worked. Many thought that the bright light and hustle and bustle of the business city was a distraction, but not Kaylee. She was energized by the city, the chaos, the constant motion.

Kaylee rarely sat at her desk; idle hands and idle feet were not her thing. She quickly responded to a few urgent phone calls and messages her assistant had left for her, delegated what she could to her team, and jumped out of her chair to work at her table.

Sarah was awesome. It was important to have a team you can count on. She reached across the table for the map she had made the night before.

Along Interstate 40 there was a clear pattern. Diving into the temporal and spatial separation, she noted that the abductions appeared to be three hundred to six hundred miles apart. That was a wide area for most serial killers. Was there a central point that they radiated from? Studying the patterns, all of her statistical tools kept saying random, but Kaylee knew nothing was ever random.

"What if I widened the search area? Let's see what pops." She pushed the enter key on her computer. Surprisingly, ten more abductions showed up, bringing her total to fifteen. She sent the list of new cases to Sarah. "Please compile these files," was all she typed in the email.

Within a few minutes, Sarah entered the room. "Good morning, Kaylee. I brought you a cup of coffee along with the files you asked for. Looks like you are deep into researching a story. Anything I can help with?"

Kaylee reached for the steaming mug of morning goodness. "I'm working on an idea of a string of missing women along Interstate 40, the major east-west interstate along the southern United States. It starts in California, just outside of Los Angeles, goes through Arizona, New Mexico, northern Texas, Oklahoma, Arkansas, Tennessee, all the way to North Carolina. It's a heavily traveled route for interstate commerce. The southern routes are preferred due to less chance of weather delays compared with northern routes."

Kaylee quickly opened the files and, looking at the pictures, she went down her checklist. Women—check. Age—various. Bodies recovered—seven.

Scratching her head, she ran her fingers through her hair, and remembered the ladies with the scarves. All of them were still missing. Their bodies were never recovered. She closed the folders of the seven cases where the bodies were recovered.

"These are out." She handed the closed folders back to Sarah. "This killer doesn't dump his bodies, or at least he doesn't like them found."

Sarah took the folders and nodded at her boss's explanation.

Kaylee's eyes darted over the information spread across the table, searching for some other clue, the little breadcrumb that no one else had noticed.

"You always say, 'Discovery is seeing what others have seen but thinking what no one has thought.'" Sarah gave a cheerful smile.

"Exactly, Sarah!" Kaylee took another sip of coffee and looked at the map. There were a few hits in North Carolina and Tennessee, but the majority of them were west of the Mississippi River. Mostly centered in Texas, New Mexico, and Arizona. Kaylee collected and quickly flipped through the folders and sifted them into piles on the table. "Ones in truck stops, these went missing from restaurants, and these were last seen getting into cars, either their own or others." Kaylee organized the files as she saw them in her mind. The largest pile was for truck stops, with a close second being restaurants. "The busiest truck stops will have on average over five thousand visitors a day. A list of all the trucks that were in these areas on the abduction dates would be thousands. We have to figure out a way to narrow it down."

She learned on her science research: Look to the outliers to find the trend. So she focused on the missing lady from North Carolina, Candice, and picked three others, two in Tennessee and one outside Chapel Hill, North Carolina, just off I-40, and pulled their files into a stack. She pushed aside the other folders to the far end of the table. "Let's focus on these few." As she began to recite what she knew of each lady, Sarah listened attentively.

"Candice was a blonde, late-twenties, pregnant, and worked as an accountant. Margaret was a redhead, early fifties, divorced, and was a waitress at a Chinese restaurant. Lucy was an Asian woman, early thirties, married with young children, owned a nail salon in eastern Tennessee. Mary, an older lady, sixty-five with blonde, obviously dyed, hair, a widow whose husband died in the line of service as a fireman. She was a stay-at-home grandmother who looked after her two grandchildren."

"It's almost time for your call about Kate from Arizona." Sarah was a master at keeping Kaylee on schedule.

Kaylee glanced at her watch and walked over to her desk as Sarah left the room. Quickly, she dialed the phone number on her notepad.

A shaky voice answered, "Hello?"

"Hi, this is Kaylee Smith-Roberts from the *Chicago Tribune*. I am looking to speak with Noelle."

"Hi, Kaylee. This is Noelle."

"Is this still a good time for you?"

"Yes, of course. I've been waiting for your call. I hope you can help us find my sister."

"I hope we find some answers for you. Let me tell you a little more about myself and then we can review what you know about your sister's disappearance. Sound good?" Her voice softened as she shifted her weight in her chair.

"Sounds perfect." Noelle's voice grew steadier.

"I work for the *Chicago Tribune* and have been a crime journalist for the past five years. I specialize in missing persons and unsolved crimes. I studied journalism as well as criminology in college and have worked with some of the best at the FBI, as well as detectives and even other reporters." She paused a moment, allowing Noelle to interject. With the silence, Kaylee continued. "I have identified a series of missing women, and I'm trying to determine if there is a relationship. I'm hoping that you can help."

"So you think this is more than just Kate?"

"I am not sure yet, but I wanted to talk with you to see if we can figure that out."

"Anything you need if it helps find Kate."

"Tell me about Kate. What did she like to do?"

"She was a great mom to her two girls. She was raising them on her own and worked hard as a teacher. She was loved by everyone and had finally started to live for herself." Her voice cracked as she talked about her sister.

"Tell me more about how she was living for herself."

"Her divorce from her husband was final about ten months before her disappearance. She struggled to find her way. After so many years of being controlled, she was just learning how to stand on her own. That is the worst thing. She was finally happy."

"I can tell you love her very much. Tell me about where she was last seen." Kaylee prodded, hoping to uncover a clue.

"She called from work as she did every day to let us know that she was on her way home. She mentioned that she was planning to make a couple of stops and to not hold dinner for her."

"What time was that?" Kaylee flipped through the file on the elementary school teacher who went missing in Sedona, Arizona.

"Around four thirty. She normally spent around an hour at school after the students were released. Since it was a Friday, it wasn't unusual for her to make a few stops on her way home."

As Kaylee studied the picture taken from the security camera as Kate exited the school, she noted the scarf she held in her hand. "Tell me about habits that Kate had, places she liked to go, clothes she liked to wear, hobbies she had."

"Funny you mentioned clothes." Noelle laughed. "Kate was obsessed with scarves. She had hundreds of them. It was her signature piece. She also admired Jackie Kennedy Onassis, President Kennedy's wife, and her iconic pillbox hats. She couldn't afford the hats and didn't have a place to store them, so she opted for scarves."

"There is definitely an air of sophistication and elegance that comes with wearing hats and scarves, isn't there?" Kaylee noted the interest in the upper-class lifestyle in her notes.

"Oh yes! Kate was the utmost of sophistication. She loved watching old movies starring Audrey Hepburn and Elizabeth Taylor. That's where I think her inspiration for the scarves came from."

"There is something about those old movies, isn't there? Not to mention the influence these women had in the postwar era."

"Kate often spoke about Liz being the sexy bombshell and Audrey being the girl next door. Back to the Ginger or Mary Ann conversations of what men prefer. Kate was definitely a 'Mary Ann.' She was an ordinary girl with great aspirations and an unparalleled skill at inspiring others to achieve their potential. That's why she was such a great teacher." Noelle's speech pattern quickened as she talked about her sister.

As she flipped through the notes, Kaylee noted something. "I see in my notes that your sister had recently been recognized for her teaching?"

"Oh yes! She was so humbled by that. Kate didn't like the spotlight, even though she frequently found herself there. She was named Teacher of the Year for the county and the state for 1991." Noelle paused before she added, "Hard to believe it's been two years since her disappearance."

"That's certainly a notable accomplishment." Kaylee focused the conversation back to Kate's behaviors. "You mentioned Kate didn't really like being the 'celebrity'?"

"No, she didn't. I think that came from her low self-confidence. Her ex-husband really did a number on her. I really hate that man. He may not have physically abused her, but the physiological scars ran deep. That's what I meant earlier, by that she finally was living her best life.

Everyone could see the change in how she carried herself. Even her scarves. She used to often cover her head with them, and they were large, heavy, dark. She wore them like cloaks, hiding from the world. Over the past months, she started wearing brightly covered, silk-like ones that fluttered in the breeze as if they were waving at people."

Kaylee sensed the pride in Noelle's words. "That's a keen observation. I can see that shift in the pictures I have of your sister. Her smile when she received the Teacher of the Year award says it all, and that red-white-and-blue scarf is beautiful."

"Thanks! I actually picked that up for her. She wanted to look like the all-American girl, and I thought that a patriotic scarf would make her outfit." Noelle's voice once again conveyed pride. "She had that scarf with her the day she disappeared."

Bingo! The linkage she was looking for. "Noelle, I have really enjoyed our conversation, and I would like to arrange to come to Sedona, Arizona, to meet you in person. Perhaps we could even arrange to speak to some of Kate's friends and coworkers. I really like to get to know the people personally that I am writing about face-to-face. Is that okay with you?"

"I would like that very much! I have spoken with so many detectives and reporters since Kate's disappearance; all have focused on the last moments of where she was, her ex-husband," Noelle excitedly responded. "No one has really tried to understand who Kate was as a person, mother, teacher. You certainly have a different approach, and if I may say, one that I prefer. When are you thinking of coming?"

"I would like to come this week. Perhaps we could have an initial meeting on Friday and then set some more things up for next week." Kaylee flipped through her datebook.

"That would work perfectly. I would want you to meet her girls as well. I'll talk to some people here and see who may be willing to talk with you."

"That would be perfect. I will have my assistant, Sarah Black, call you back with my travel plans, and she can help work with you on putting together a schedule. I am looking forward to meeting you and getting to know the woman behind the scarf," Kaylee added with a laugh.

A laugh came from the phone as well. "Touché, Kaylee. I feel like you know her already. You share her sense of humor," Noelle said. "Kaylee? One more thing. Thank you. Thank you for caring to get to know my sister. I am looking forward to the first articles that will be an awesome tribute to the legacy she left behind and an inspiration to her daughters and her students."

"My pleasure. My approach is unconventional, to say the least. My success lies in the space in between the facts. Seeing what others have seen but thinking what no one has thought," Kaylee stated as she smiled. "We will figure out what happened to your sister. I have a good feeling about this. We will talk soon."

As the infamous click was heard ending their conversation, Kaylee studied Kate's file, added notes from her conversation with Noelle, then closed the file and walked over to her table.

As if on cue, Sarah walked in. "Looks like you had a good conversation with Noelle?"

Embarrassed, Kaylee lowered her head and laughed. "My awesome poker face gives me away every time."

"What do they say? Lucky at cards, unlucky in love, or something like that." Sarah laughed as well.

"Well, apparently I am unlucky at both. Maybe one day, I'll find the Clyde to my Bonnie. Someone who will appreciate my obsession with unsolved mysteries and what's lurking behind the corner of the dark alley."

"You will find your prince charming." Sarah changed the subject back to the case. "So are you headed to Arizona?"

"Yes. Can you book flights for this week returning end of next week? I told Noelle we would connect briefly Friday, and then I'll talk to others the following week." Kaylee was grateful that Sarah required minimal direction. "Let's get back to studying these files. I think I may have another thread or two."

Kaylee and Sarah continued to study the files, desperate to detect the breadcrumbs. "This could be our big break," Kaylee said, desperate to find the thread. "This could be the one that finally gets us noticed."

Sarah nodded. "Your dream of being a nationally recognized private investigator is within your grasp!"

"Exactly! And maybe I'll find my soulmate lurking in a dark corner of the desert as a bonus!" They both laughed.

~ CHAPTER 5 ~

WESTBOUND

It was time to get back on the road. Curtis rolled into the truck yard. He jumped out of his Mustang and grabbed his travel bag out of the trunk. Casually, he walked up to the door to the transportation office.

"Hi, Curtis!" a familiar voice said from behind the reception desk.

"Good morning, Barb. How is the most beautiful lady at Hughes doing this fine morning?" He leaned on the reception counter and smirked.

"Oh honey, if I had a dollar for every time some hot young stud called me beautiful, I wouldn't be working here anymore!" Barb drawled, her Southern accent strong. Barbara Hughes was the founder's daughter and ran the trucking company with her husband. The Hugheses and the MacIntyres had known each other for generations.

"But none as adorable as me!" he responded with his trademark eyebrow tic. "What route did I draw today?"

"I gave you the one to Phoenix. I'll have to find you a backhaul in a few days. Thought you might could use a few days to hang out in the desert before returning." Barb handed him his bill of lading and weighing and inspection.

"You do know me well, lady." Curtis grabbed his bag and headed out the side door to the truck yard. Walking to the blue Peterbilt super cab, Curtis's pulse picked up as he reached to grab the shiny silver bar of his rig and swing himself up to open the door. As he settled into the familiar seat, the air springs sighed under his weight. He placed his bag in the back and pushed the starter. The engine roared to life. His trailer was already hooked up. "Let's get to it."

He shifted the big rig into gear, and the engine labored under the weight of the trailer. Expertly maneuvering the rig out of the yard, he blew the air horn as he rolled out to the main road. This was a trucker's rite of passage, a signal to Barb that he was rolling.

Driving west towards Greensboro, North Carolina, Curtis had his window cracked just a little. His morning coffee sat in the holder next to his Boston cream donut, courtesy of Barb. Oh, she loved to spoil him since his mom passed. Barb and his mom, Deb, were best friends. They grew up together, raised their children as cousins, and never thought that one would be gone so suddenly. It had been a decade since Mom's death, and in some ways it seemed like a lifetime ago and other times just yesterday.

Curtis started driving for the Hughes after his mother's passing. It was a way for him to escape the constant reminder at the farm. It gave him an opportunity to be alone with his thoughts, to process what had happened, as Susan always said. Over the past few years, Susan and Curtis had grown apart. Susan went off to college, and Curtis took to the open road. These two lifestyles appeared to be mutually exclusive. They still would connect when he was in town, a quick meal, chats, and general catching up with what was going on in each other's lives. Their connection was strong but no longer exclusive. They were both okay with that. "The best of both worlds," Susan liked to say.

Curtis tuned in the country station and began singing along to "Chattahoochee" by Alan Jackson. Even though the song had not been on the charts for several years, it was still played regularly on the radio.

He loved being on the road, connecting with his thoughts. It was meditative for him, a spiritual connection with the Universe. Even as a young teen, he used to love riding the tractor around the farm and up and down the road. He and Susan would drive for hours around the countryside in the Mustang, music blasting, not saying a word, just being in the moment.

Bound for Phoenix, he had a few days to hang out while his rebound trip was finalized. Barb always did know when he was in need of a break. It was the mother instinct in her. Women, especially mothers, always had this sixth sense, maternal intuition. They knew what their family members needed sometimes before they did. He smiled as he remembered how he felt when his mother did that.

As he drove down the westbound interstate, he breathed in the fresh spring air, watching the blooms of the Bradford pear trees and the mass plantings of Stella d'Oro lilies that lined the highways. North Carolina always did an awesome job with the roadside foliage. The last of the rosebud blooms were fading, making way for the second show.

Hours later, Curtis headed into Tennessee on his way to Nashville. Keeping a careful eye on his log since he could only drive eleven hours a day according to federal law. He was a stickler about making sure his logs were unchallenged if scrutinized. He figured out where he would need to stop for a rest and refuel. It looked like Nashville was the likely target for his next meal. He set his cruise control at seventy-five—it was a seventy-mile-per-hour zone after all—and turned on the CB radio as a distraction. The road sure could get lonely, and he liked to connect with his fellow comrades in arms over the airwaves.

"Breaker, breaker one nine, this is the Sandman rolling into the Volunteer State. Any of my fellow comrades out there got your ears on? Come on back." Curtis spoke into his CB mic. He let off the button and waited for the static hiss to be broken by a familiar voice.

"Hey, Sandman, this is the Chantilly Kid. Good to hear your voice. I'm rolling westbound on 40 at marker 14. Was clear from the line with no bears in sight. Planning to break at the stop at Nashville if you want to grab a bite," came a voice from the speaker.

Curtis had met the Chantilly Kid when they were in driving school. He hailed from a small town, Chantilly, Virginia, and Curtis was from a similar town in North Carolina. They hit it off from the start, and they liked to throw back a beer or two and shoot the shit.

"Hey, Kid, good to hear from you. I'm looking to stop on the other side of Nashville so that works. I got a couple of beers in the cab and am planning on hunkering down for the night as well. Let's plan on it. I'll ping you on the radio when I get closer. Peace out, brother."

"Hey, this is Big Daddy. Got room in your posse for one more?" barked another voice from the abyss.

"Absolutely," responded Curtis. "The more, the merrier! Might need to refill my cooler as you jokers will no doubt clear me out."

"No doubt, no doubt!" responded the Chantilly Kid. "I got a few bottles myself, so I will contribute to the festivities."

Big Daddy laughed. "Can always count on you youngsters to supply the purchased stuff. I got my special essential oils. Being Tennessee born and bred, don't leave home without 'em."

"Heard that, Big Daddy. Well, we may have to check out those essential oils, now won't we? See you all in a few, over and out." Curtis chuckled.

The three gentlemen enjoyed a nice meal, joked with the waitress, and swapped stories for over an hour. It's good to share time with friends and family, Curtis sighed, thinking about past times.

Curtis's mother, Debra, always had been a big fan of quality time and making memories. Some nights when they would gather around the dinner table, Curtis and his dad had been amazed at how she seemed to know when they needed the comfort provided by their favorite meal because they were feeling a little down or when a fun night of fondue or making your own pizzas would hit the spot. The ladies in his family definitely possessed a higher-than-average emotional intelligence. It seemed almost telepathic. Deb could just look at Curtis or Dad and instinctually know what they were thinking before they even said it. She had a way of expertly knowing when to remain silent, when to offer a supportive touch, and when to offer advice. His grandma had the same instincts. They were cut from the same cloth, kindred spirits, if you will. Curtis would often joke with his mom about her crystals, candles, oils, and scents that she would use to maintain balance in the house and in her family.

"You are part witch, Mom," Curtis would say when she would walk in his room with that burning bunch of sage used to remove the evil spirts and cleanse the mind and house.

"It is not witchcraft, Curtis. My motherly intuition says that the juju in here is not to my liking." She'd meet his snide remark with her own quick wit.

"My juju is just fine, Mom," Curtis insisted.

"If it's so fine, then why are you struggling? The demons are near, Curtis."

Curtis snapped to attention at his mother's response. Did she know his thoughts? Could she read his mind? He never talked of the demons or the thoughts that often filled his head. Sure everyone knew that he and Susan were preoccupied with death and serial killers, but did anyone know what truly went on inside his head? He had never acted on the urges, but they were getting stronger. The paranoia was real. It was very real. Curtis needed to cleanse his thoughts of the demons. His mom taught him this. Even after her death, Curtis continued to have wrapped sage so that he could have better clarity in his path.

~ CHAPTER 6 ~

A Corner in Arizona

Curtis always loved to spend time checking out the local culture. One thing was for sure, Curtis loved people watching. He jumped in his rental car, a silver Nissan Altima. "We aren't in Kansas anymore, and this certainly isn't my Mustang." He cringed a little when he heard the little four-cylinder turbo engine give off that high-pitched whine. It would suffice to get him from point A to point B, and the price was right. Off he went from the Phoenix airport heading up the interstate through Sedona towards Flagstaff. He had rented a little two-bedroom house in downtown Flagstaff for the next four days and would use that as his home base. It would give him the opportunity to travel around a bit and soak in some of the local history and mingle with the people of the desert Southwest.

The two-hour drive from Phoenix to Flagstaff gave him a chance to clear his head and refocus. Having four days to hang out was a rarity, and he looked forward to the downtime. As he left the low desert of Phoenix behind, the landscape of the mid desert took shape through the windshield of the Nissan. The red rocks of Sedona appeared in the distance, and the brush of the desert started to get taller. Leaving the sweltering valley of Phoenix for the red rock of Sedona was a rite of passage. Like a walk through time, the red rock faded and, as he continued to climb in altitude, the high desert began to take shape.

A little after three p.m., he turned onto Hill Road and followed the directions to the little blue house on Prairie Street. He parked the car, grabbed his bag, and headed inside. It had been a long day, and he looked forward to relaxing in front of the TV, ordering pizza, and hanging out by the pool. He planned to head to Winslow in the morning.

He looked up at the bright Arizona sun. He could get used to this life. He closed his eyes and stretched out on the chaise beside the small pool at his vacation rental. As he laid there, his thoughts wandered back to happier times. He missed the connection he shared with Susan. If there was such a thing as a soulmate, was she his? He wasn't sure if he would ever truly have a "normal" relationship with a woman. After the pain his mother endured and how his father treated her, Curtis knew what he didn't want, but what was it that he did?

His dark side further compounded things as he had unleashed the monster inside himself, averaging a kill a month, sometimes more. Like Pandora's box, once released, it could not be contained. When people said, "to thine own self be true," that conjured up a whole different level for him. The Mason blood coursed through his veins, and although he justified his actions, the fact remained that he was a killer.

He enjoyed the hunt, the kill, watching the fear in their eyes change to acceptance as they realized that their time in this world was ending and was unpreventable. That final acceptance was where he obtained his gratification. Knowing he was able to save them from future pain that they might endure, from experiencing the desperate situation that drove his mother to end her own life.

He could never fathom how pain like that felt. To be dead, to leave your only son motherless, to sever all ties with this earthly world and cross over into an unknown black abyss, the finality of it all was immense. To have a pain so great that the more viable option was to kill herself rather than endure the emotional turmoil any longer. Had his mother gone through that? No one should have to endure that level of pain.

That was his calling, to save women from suffering that pain. He would make the decision for them; he would help them peacefully cross over into the abyss where there was no more pain. We all should be so lucky.

He opened his eyes and watched the sun start its slow descent behind the hills. It painted the sky with reds, pinks, and oranges. He couldn't help but think of his mother, who loved to watch the sunrises and sunsets. "This one's for you, Mom." He lifted his beer towards the sun. "And to finding someone that gets me like you do."

A few miles away, sitting on the rooftop pool at the Hilton, Kaylee sipped on a blue Hawaiian, her signature cocktail. The sun blazed a mass of colors, a volcano erupting in the western sky. As she contemplated her next steps in investigating the unsolved disappearances along Interstate 40, she ran through the conversations with Noelle earlier in the day, her mind kept circling back to the question: Who was the person she was searching for, and what would she do when she found him? It wasn't a matter of *if*, it was a matter of *when*. She had learned years ago to sometimes give in to her thoughts and let them take her where she needed to go.

It was all about the journey. The destination was the reward at the end. Her killer was the reward. What journey was she on? Was this more personal than it seemed? Was this trip actually going to help her find herself, her greater purpose?

She struggled to fit in and yearned for that sense of belonging that so many of her friends talked about. Where did she belong? Was she destined to travel this life alone, solo, always chasing the bread crumbs left by others?

"I will leave the crumbs for others to follow. I will have a partner by my side to walk this journey with. I will find my soulmate." Kaylee said these affirmations out loud. If she put it out in the Universe, it would become a self-fulfilling prophecy. She believed in the Law of Attraction, of manifesting her destiny. She wanted this to be, she needed this to be, but was she ready to accept it if it came to be?

As the sky grew dark and the stars shone bright, Kaylee headed back to her room. The next morning, she headed out on I-40 across the desert towards Winslow. It was about a two-hour drive to the Hopi Indian Ruins at Homolovi State Park. This excursion was just the thing she needed to clear her mind. She had spent the last two days before her trip in intense preparation for the interviews with various detectives, witnesses, family members, and friends of missing people during her days in the Southwest desert.

It was draining to talk to the victims' family and friends. The glimmer of hope in their eyes as they hung on each question she asked, as they searched frantically for a clue that she knew where their loved one was, that they were still alive and would be reunited. As she pulled into Winslow and got out to walk around the town, she recited her affirmations once more. "I will leave the crumbs for others to follow. I will have a partner by my side to walk this journey with. I will find my soulmate. A face to the image in my dreams." With her last words still lingering in the air, she took a deep breath of the desert air, straightened her back, smiled, and headed off towards the center of town.

As she got closer to that famous corner in Winslow, Arizona, she couldn't stop herself, and sang as the statue of the Eagles and the flatbed Ford came into view. Not realizing she was actually singing "Take It Easy" out loud, she jumped when a voice from behind her joined in perfect harmony.

As she turned around, their eyes met, and both laughed. Those piercing blue eyes, that dark hair, and those muscles accentuated by a snug T-shirt. He was a work of art sparking Kaylee's curiosity. "You have a beautiful voice," was all she managed to say, hoping he didn't notice her obvious attraction for him.

"Well, thanks, but I only sing for fun. Besides, who doesn't like the Eagles? I don't think you could mess those lyrics up, especially not in this town or on this corner. That song is timeless." He motioned to the truck and statue. "Plus, with such a beautiful lady for inspiration." His words hung in the air, punctuated by a quick flick of his eyebrow and a smile that crept across his lips.

Oh, he was good. This was not his first rodeo. Kaylee stepped back, tilting her head as she judged him. She decided to play along, as this wasn't her first trip around the block either. "Well, likewise. My name is Kaylee, and I am in town from Chicago for work and just getting out for the day to see some of the sites." She searched for a companion of this handsome man that might spoil her plans.

"Hi, Kaylee. My name is Curtis, and I, too, am in town for work and taking in some of the local history as well."

"That's great!" Quickly realizing she was a little too exuberant, she swallowed and added in an even tone, "Maybe we can hang together, if you are by yourself."

"I just happen to be flying solo this trip. And I would love the company of such a beautiful woman for the day, maybe longer…" he added with a wink and a smile.

She laughed like a giddy schoolgirl and gazed up at this handsome man. "Let's just start with today and see how it goes." She gave him her own coy look.

"Shall we?" Curtis motioned towards the truck parked on the famous corner of Route 66.

They both walked towards the corner to read the historic plaque and look at the statues of the Eagles.

Playing up the whole tourist vibe, Kaylee pulled out a disposable camera, and they asked tourists to snap their picture leaning on the truck and posing like they were longtime friends, not strangers whose paths just crossed serendipitously.

Kaylee knew nothing in this world was truly by chance; everything was part of a carefully calculated plan. She put her inquisitive mind aside to be present in the moment. They both chatted so effortlessly as they walked through the town and dodged in and out of various souvenir shops, looking at memorabilia, Native American garb, and Winslow tchotchkes. Every store they went into seemed to be playing Eagles music.

After a few hours, Curtis said, "If I hear 'Hotel California' one more time, I'm going to smack someone."

Kaylee's immediate laughter showed her empathic agreement to his declaration.

As they continued to shop and look around the town, she glanced at her watch. "Gosh, it's almost two. No wonder I'm feeling a little hungry. Maybe we should grab something to eat? I think I remember seeing a pub back by the truck."

"I think you're right."

As they wandered back towards the center of town, they spied the pub, walked in, and sat in one of the booths.

"So tell me about Chicago." Curtis held the menu but focused on her.

"I love the city. There is always something going on. So much history there. Lots of stories: Al Capone, Mrs. O'Leary's cow, stories of love and death, mystery and intrigue. I work for a newspaper. My office is right on Michigan Avenue overlooking the Chicago River." Kaylee moved her hands around as she punctuated key points.

"Oh, a lady from the high-rent district." Curtis raised his chin, pointing his nose upwards. "I'm just a simple country boy from North Carolina. I grew up on a farm and now I drive a truck."

"I didn't grow up with a silver spoon, that's for sure. My father wasn't in my life, but my stepfather was, and that came with its own challenges." Kaylee rolled her eyes.

"Childhood wasn't that great? I'm sure you got into your fair share of trouble. I can see you may have a little rebel streak hidden under all that sophisticated upper-northside exterior."

"Oh? And I can say the same for you, Mr. MacIntyre. There's many facets to you as well."

"Touché, my dear. You can read me like a book." As the words left his mouth, they both laughed.

"Of course I can. I'm a writer," Kaylee batted back. "So why did you decide to follow a life on the road?"

"I enjoy the autonomy that it gives. I like to be independent. My life is somewhat of a solo mission, or at least so far," he added as Kaylee detected a slight hint of hope in his tone. "Maybe you will be the one that changes all that."

Kaylee looked past his blue eyes, straight into his soul. Her eyes widened as she caught a glimpse of what lay behind his charming exterior. "I do like a challenge, but I'm not a miracle worker. I have seen beauty in people who were called ugly, and I have seen the devil in the most angelic faces. I also know firsthand the devastation when someone told you 'we're in this together' or 'I got you' then abandoned you, leaving you to pick up the pieces when the shit gets real, leaving you to handle your part and their part too."

His mouth fell open at her words.

"Why the shocked look?"

"It's like you are inside my head. That you can read my thoughts." The shocked expression continued as he spoke. "What is the story behind the green-eyed creature that apparently can read minds?"

"Now, what would be the fun in that?" She teased him along. "A girl needs to keep a little mystery. Glad to see you are intrigued by my secrets." She smiled momentarily and dropped her guard, allowing him to see her vulnerability and enter her mind if he wanted.

"Everyone has secrets. Some are just better at hiding them." Curtis leaned back and furrowed his brow.

In response to his caution, Kaylee studied his thoughts, searched his heart for clues before she responded. "Like the parent that abandoned you by choice, or the one that caused it, or the stranger that traded sexual intimacy but was never offered a safe haven that honored your heart. From the friendships and family who always took more than they ever gave. A wall was built. A strong wall that shielded your heart from abuse, neglect, betrayal, and disappointment from those who could not or would not be there for you."

"Are you some type of witch?" He pushed back against the table like he was trying to increase the distance between them.

Kaylee knew she had struck a nerve. The raw emotion that erupted from him was intense, rhythmically spewing forth like arterial blood, each beat sending it high into the air. Not truly sure if she was referring to what she saw in Curtis or if she was talking about herself. Love was something they both yearned for. "Trust is something that must be earned. To trust, one needs hope. To trust is to be vulnerable. But no matter how you dress it up and display it proudly to make it seem like independence, it is what you always wanted. In truth, it's your wounded, scarred, broken heart behind that protective brick wall."

Curtis leaned forward. "Impenetrable. Nothing gets in. No hurt gets in. But no love gets in either."

"Or out," Kaylee stated in a hushed tone. "Fortresses and armor are for those in battle."

"Or for those who believe the battle is coming," Curtis contended. "Right?"

"True, but sometimes there is a chink in the armor, and sometimes a spark of vulnerability escapes. And if the right person is there to see it, it may make all the difference." Kaylee reached across the table and placed her fingers gently on his hand.

Curtis pulled back his hand with a sharp twitch.

Kaylee's fingers curled up and retracted slightly as she patiently waited for his next move. She closed her eyes slightly.

Curtis relaxed, laid his hand flat on the table, outstretched fingers reaching towards her hand and muttered, "Sorry, you startled me."

"No worries, Curtis." Her hand gently covered his.

The waitress came up. "Have you decided?"

They never separated their hands as they placed their orders. Kaylee felt the energy between them and didn't want to break that flow. Was his the face she longed to see?

Their conversation continued but focused on more lighthearted topics as they enjoyed their meal.

As they finished, the waitress returned. "Do you need anything else?"

"No, I think we have everything." Kaylee gave Curtis a quick wink and squeezed his hand tight, her fingers intertwined with his.

"Okay then, I'll just leave this with you. No rush. Whenever you are ready." She looked through the checks, selected the correct one, and placed it on the table.

There was something about Curtis, something she couldn't quite put her finger on. He was different than other men. They couldn't come from more different backgrounds but somehow they seem to connect. The attraction between them was obvious, not only to them but everyone around them.

Curtis appeared to be lost in thought, but Kaylee spoke. "I heard there are local ruins just outside Winslow."

"Yes, I read about those as well. I think there are pueblos too. It's just down the road a few minutes. Homolovi State Park."

"Homo love what?" Kaylee gave a bewildered laugh.

"Homo-love-ee, Kaylee. I think it is just what the doctor ordered for us. A little love would do us both some good, don't you think?"

"I think it is exactly the right treatment for what ails us, a Native American ruin built by the Hopi tribe would be quite the adventure." She laid both her hands on his. "It's fate, Curtis. The Universe showed us what we needed. It's our responsibility to do it."

"We can't disappoint the Universe, now can we?" He picked up the bill.

Kaylee reached for her wallet.

He quickly said, "Oh no, honey. This one is on me."

Kaylee smiled and lowered her head. *Honey.* Was that just a Southern thing, or was there something more?

Time would tell, but for now, they were heading to the state park and would spend the rest of the afternoon hiking around the ruins, looking for pottery shards, and soaking up the local heritage and culture. Maybe Curtis was her soulmate. She couldn't help but think about her conversation with Sarah back in Chicago. Could he be the one for her? She had put it out into the Universe.

He walked towards the door, bidding a good day to the waitress and bartender. He reached for the door. "After you, my lady."

"Why, thank you." She sashayed through the door, grabbing her sunglasses off her head and placing them over her eyes. The Arizona sun was strong, especially for this Chicago girl.

Curtis led the way towards his silver Nissan Altima. "Your chariot, my lady." He opened the passenger door, and Kaylee slid in.

"Thank you, kind sir," she responded with her best British accent, and they both laughed as Curtis skipped around the car and jumped into the driver's seat.

"Too bad this isn't my Mustang back home. It would surely put a smile on your face as it threw you back into your seat."

"Hmm. Might just have to take a trip to North Carolina to experience that."

~ CHAPTER 7 ~

HISTORY BEGINS

As Curtis and Kaylee traveled towards Homolovi, they chatted about cultural differences and how Native Americans valued age and wisdom that elders possessed, the importance of family, and the respect of nature and the earth's resources.

"It's sad that we don't value those things as much today as in the past," Kaylee concluded.

"I agree. There is so much wisdom to be gained from our elders. I love sitting around the campfire, hearing the stories of years ago from my grandfather and his friends. That is where we come from and who we are. Their stories represent our lifeblood, our family folklore. It really should be preserved and shared with future generations," Curtis responded.

"I couldn't agree more." She looked out the window.

Where did this guy come from? He appeared out of nowhere, and he was somehow inside her thoughts. He said things as his own ideas, but she could have said them herself. Was he psychic? Could he read her mind? Was this what it meant to meet your soulmate? Until that moment, she wasn't sure soulmates actually existed. Now she found herself questioning whether a virtual stranger she only met a few hours ago was hers. What was going on with her?

She needed to get a grip on her emotions. Was this a physical attraction just misinterpreted as something more? Love at first sight did not exist in her reality, but then again, nothing about this day was her normal.

As they reached the state park, Curtis broke the silence. "Here we are. Let's head to the visitor center and check out what is here, shall we?"

"Sounds like a plan."

They both got out of the car and headed down the walkway towards the visitor center. The cool air inside the building refreshed them after the hot, desert sun. As they entered the exhibits, a park ranger approached and told them about the site and the historical significance. As they chatted effortlessly with the ranger, asking about the family and tribe structures, how they lived, what they ate, several other visitors entered the building.

"The Hopi tribe that inhabited this area were villagers and farmers. The name Hopi means peaceful ones," the ranger expertly explained. "Each Hopi village was divided into clans governed by a chief, the spiritual leader of the village. The villagers lived in adobe houses known as pueblos. There were multiple levels made of adobe, or clay and straw baked into hard bricks. The Hopi tribes believe that the Universe and all natural objects—animals, plants, trees, rivers, mountains, rocks, etc.—have souls or spirits. The tribe believes in the kachina concept, which had three different aspects:

the supernatural being or spirit and deities, the kachina dancers, and kachina dolls."

"Doesn't each kachina hold different powers?" Curtis asked.

"Yes, they do," the ranger agreed. "Kokopelli is the most famous and is often depicted as a hunchbacked, dancing flute player wearing antlers or horns on his head. In Native American traditions, antlers and horns signified spiritual power." As he continued, a small crowd gathered to listen.

A man with a baseball hat and red sneakers asked, "What does the Kokopelli represent?"

"This legendary supernatural creature represents fertility and brought a sense of security and well-being to the people, assuring their success in hunting, growing crops, and in human conception."

"What about the family units of the Hopi people?" Kaylee asked.

"Family and ancestors were very important, then and now. The Hopi tribe believe they are the guardians of their rites and knowledge of their ancestors. There is a well-known quote, 'We are like pottery shards right now, all broken up. But when we get together, we are all one.' This to me exemplifies the Hopi culture. They value community and helping the people in their community. They didn't see it as charity; it was their purpose." The ranger pointed out items in the visitor center museum.

"My late mother always said that each person comes into your life for a reason. Some are always with you and are family. Some are like passing ships that are there for a short time and are quickly forgotten. Some are friends who we make along the way, and no matter how long they stay, it always seems too short. Each one teaches you something you need on your journey." Curtis reached for Kaylee's hand.

"Most indigenous people share a similar belief. The Universe gave you what you needed when you needed it. Those gifts come in many forms. The people you meet along your journey definitely play a critical role in your destiny," the ranger responded.

Kaylee stood motionless, speechless as she absorbed the impact of what she heard. The excitement of this historical sacred land showed in the sparkle in Curtis's eyes.

He squeezed Kaylee's hand. "Let's go, babe."

It felt so natural, like it was meant to be, that Kaylee willingly followed him out the door and into the bright sunshine. She was happy. For the first time in a very long time, she felt completely safe, content, and happy as a piece of the wall she had erected crumbled.

They spent the rest of the afternoon around the ruins. They read markers about the various ruins and dug in the sand for pottery shards. As the sun started setting, they headed back to the visitor center where the car was parked. They planned on heading over to the La Mesa Familiar, a historical railroad hotel built in the 1920s that had been transformed into a living museum and dining area in the main building.

"I'm excited to see La Mesa Familiar. So glad you found it," she said as they neared the car.

"La Mesa Familiar means family table in Spanish. That place has quite the history. It dates back to when the railroad was first built," Curtis added.

The family table seemed fitting for them. Two virtual strangers who found comfort and security with each other. Someone had accepted them at face value and gave them a safe place to drop their masks, to share a meal.

Kaylee and Curtis pulled into the parking lot. They were early and planned to look around the gift shop and check out this local landmark before their meal.

As they walked towards the main entrance, a steel-blue minivan careened towards them only to whip into a handicapped spot, its front wheels hitting the parking bumper and bouncing to a stop. The driver's door flew open and an old Native American lady popped out dressed in a long tunic, leggings, and sneakers.

Kaylee and Curtis came to a complete stop and stood there watching, speechless.

"Excuse me. Excuse me. Do you have a minute to talk?" the older lady shouted as she slid open the back door of the van and clambered around in the seat, coming out with a green woven satchel that she flung over her shoulder, her head dipped under the strap so it hung across her body. She scurried over to them. "I sell some of the sage from my garden and donate the money to my local Hopi tribe to help us get by. Are you guys local?"

"No. We are from North Carolina and are in town visiting," Curtis responded.

"Do you know anything about the Hopi tribe native to this area?" the lady asked.

"Yes. We just spent the day touring the ruins at Homolovi State Park outside of Winslow. Very interesting. We learned about the Hopi culture and looked at all the artifacts and pottery pieces that you could find at the dig sites," Kaylee said, unsure why this woman crossed their paths. What was her purpose? This whole day had been full of twists and turns and unexpected events. She was both excited and nervous at the same time.

"Did you go to the Hopi Reservation to see the pueblos? It is only about fifteen minutes farther but much better and bigger for understanding how the tribes lived."

"No. We weren't aware of that site. Wish we could have gone there. It is truly fascinating to learn about how native people lived in this area," Kaylee offered.

"You would love it, dear. It's so much better than Homolovi. Anyway, like I was saying, I am selling these sage bundles from my own garden to raise money for the tribe. Would this be something you may be interested in?"

"My mom always had sage in the house. She would use it to cleanse our house and our minds," Curtis said, with a quizzical look on his face.

What special memory was linked with the sage? Kaylee tried to search his mind. Curtis looked her in the eyes, squeezed her hand. "Not now."

Shocked, Kaylee stepped back, dropping his hand. Could he read her mind as well? Who was this man?

"How much is it?" Curtis asked.

"Oh, dear, whatever you want to donate is fine. I don't have a minimal amount." She smiled.

Curtis reached for his wallet in his back pocket and opened it. "Hmm." He looked through the bills. "I'm sure you don't take cards?"

"No, cash only."

His sense of humor didn't translate very well as he reached for the ten-dollar bill and handed it to her.

"Oh my, sir. That is most generous of you. Let me find you a nice one." She sorted through the satchel, coming out with a bundle of sage bound with teal-and-white floss over a foot long. "This is the best one I have!" She handed it to Curtis.

"Let me show you how to use it. You light it and allow the smoke to float towards your face. Breathe in, cleansing your body. Circle your head with the smoke so your thoughts are pure." She moved the sage bunch in a circular motion above her head. "Circle it under each of your feet so your path is clear." She balanced on one foot then the other, circling the end of the sage bunch under each foot. "And finally circle it by each of your hands so that your actions are pure and unobstructed." She swished the sage wand over each of her palms. "That's it. You will be protected and will have purpose and vision that will carry you forward in your journey."

"Thank you so much," Curtis said. "Take care of yourself, and I hope our donation helps the Hopi tribe."

"Oh yes, sir. It will. You are both most generous and good things will come to both of you. I can see it. You have quite a journey ahead."

They parted ways and headed toward the resort entrance as she headed back to her van.

"Curtis," Kaylee said. "She saw you coming a mile away. They say a sucker is born every minute."

"I'm not a sucker, Kaylee. The Universe will bring you what you need when you need it. Obviously, one of us needed some sage and spiritual cleansing. Wonder which of us it is?" He punctuated it with his signature eyebrow nod as they both burst out in laughter.

"Which one indeed," Kaylee wondered out loud as she contemplated why he mentioned the Universe. Did he read her mind?

They enjoyed a marvelous dinner and headed back to Winslow for Kaylee to get her car. As they were saying their goodbyes, they realized they were both staying in

Flagstaff. They decided to call it a night but agreed to connect tomorrow.

Climbing into bed, Kaylee thought about the day. There was something about him that she just couldn't put her finger on. He was attractive, smart, and had a great sense of humor, but there was something else. It was even more compelling than any previous relationship. It was like they shared a deeper purpose.

As she replayed the day's conversation, Kaylee's thoughts kept drifting back to her conversation with Sarah. *You will find your prince charming* was what she had said. Kaylee remembered her response vividly. *And my soulmate lurking in a dark corner of the desert as a bonus.* Was Curtis the bonus she was hoping for? Could they share a divine purpose? Were they destined to carve a single mark on the world? They definitely shared a passion for cultures, personal motivations, and spirituality. The Universe had a way of giving you what you needed when you needed it. What was Curtis's purpose? Was he going to have a more pivotal role in her life? Why now? So many questions.

Kaylee stretched out on the hotel bed and placed the lit sage brush they purchased from the Hopi tribe lady in a glass on the nightstand. As she inhaled the sweet aroma of the burning plant, she allowed her mind to clear and focus. As she continued the spiritual cleansing process described to them, a vision in her mind's eye came into clear focus.

First, it was merely an outline, then it solidified into a clear, recognizable face, his face. She finally was able to put a name to the face: Curtis MacIntyre. She had had visions of a man since she could remember. He was always a nameless, faceless man, but someone she knew would change her life. She was never sure how or when. What she did know was that he would appear at the right time, and her purpose would become clear. What was this mysterious man from North Carolina supposed to teach her? The thought not only intrigued but delighted her. And he could read her mind as she could read his.

~ CHAPTER 8 ~

Worth, Scarves, and Secrets

Curtis awoke before dawn the next day ready to start this next chapter. His reflections the night before gave him clarity on what his next steps were. He sensed an urgency to stay with her, to protect her, to stay close to her. Curtis struggled internally as he argued within his mind. He saw the surprise on her face when he responded verbally to her mind tricks. She had recoiled. He had let her in his world for a moment earlier in the day and showed her his pain from losing his mother. The walls he built were strong and impenetrable. Could she see beyond what he wanted her to see? There was something special about Kaylee Smith-Roberts. He needed to connect with her today, but before that, he needed to take care of his urge. The family business beckoned him.

Curtis headed towards the truck yard two hours south in Phoenix where his rig was parked; he needed to get an early start on the day's activities. As he pulled into the yard, he knew this would be a quick adventure; he didn't have a lot of time. He climbed into the cab and headed down the interstate towards the north. As he approached a truck stop, he maneuvered into the parking lots. He still had his empty trailer in tow, so he blended in well in the nearly full lot.

As he gathered his stuff, he saw an older lady, probably in her mid-forties, wandering through the aisles. She was wearing jeans and a red shirt with a white scarf blowing in the wind. The scarf was thin and sheer, like an angelic wrap encircling her thin neck.

Curtis longed to touch the fabric to feel the silk slide across his fingertips. It was elegant and understated and reminded him of his mother. "Accessories should make a statement but not shout," she would say as she finalized her outfits and checked her appearance in the hall tree mirror before she exited the house for the day. "Curtis, remember, appearances matter. You need to look the part."

Curtis always took pride in his appearance and noticed others that did as well. He realized that those women who drew his attention also provoked interest from many suitors. With so many potential partners vying for their attention, surely they had more than their fair share of heartache. He often wondered if they, too, had been wronged as his mother had, if the partner they chose to commit their life to had broken that vow, that trust, and committed the ultimate betrayal.

Timing his exit from his rig, his feet hit the ground just as she was approaching the front of the cab. "Good morning." He turned from the truck.

"Good morning. How are you doing?" she replied almost automatically.

"Very well. It's a beautiful morning. Nice breeze too. I couldn't help but notice your lovely scarf. My late mother often wore sheer silk scarves like that."

She stopped, touched her scarf, and shyly looked up at him. "Thank you so much. This was a present from my former mother-in-law. She also loved scarves. She was the nicest woman. So loving and dedicated to her family. I only wish her son had inherited that quality. My condolences on the loss of your mother."

Bingo. The dead mother card always made ladies feel safe, and they would let their guards down much quicker. He glanced at his watch, noted there was not a lot of time, so he moved this along. "I'm sorry that you had to experience a bad relationship. Those are always hard. I know it sounds cliché, but not all men are assholes. Some of us are actually quite charming," he added with a chuckle and his signature eyebrow tic. He had a sixth sense in identifying women who were in bad relationships. Be it infidelity, physical or emotional abuse, it wasn't important. What was important was their suffering, silent and lonely. He had helped seventy-four other women escape this torment, and this was his lucky number seventy-five.

She laughed along with him. "Sometimes things don't always end as you hoped. That's for sure."

"I know that one. I have lived that one. Heartache is one of the worst pains one can endure. It is something I wish I could just eradicate from this reality."

"Amen to that. My name is Carol. I was just heading to grab a breakfast sandwich. Care to join me?"

"Absolutely. It would be my pleasure, Carol. And my name is Curtis."

The two wandered off towards the building to grab their sandwiches and return back to the parking lot. "I have a couple of chairs in the rig, if you would be so kind to help me grab them?"

"Of course."

Being the gentleman that he was, Curtis motioned to Carol to climb in first and followed behind to catch her if she slipped. Once inside the cab, he motioned to the back bunk. "They are just under the bunk."

Carol innocently walked back, and before she could turn around, his hands reached around and tightened her scarf around her neck. She reached up and grabbed her scarf as she struggled to breathe. Her body thrashed as she gasped for air.

He pushed her down on the bed facing the small mirror that hung at the end. He needed to see her face, to look into her eyes as she realized her destiny, as she finally accepted that she would die today, at this very minute.

As the silk noose dug into her neck, crushing her trachea, he expertly wrapped the ends of the scarf around his fists so he had more leverage. With his knee in her back between her shoulder blades, he pulled his elbow back, tightening the material around her delicate neck.

She struggled less and less, her eyes showing the small red dots as the pressure built up and the tiny blood vessels popped, one by one. Gazing into her eyes, he quietly whispered, "You will never have to endure heartache again, Carol. I am setting you free from that pain."

The tears welled in her eyes, and finally, that look of peace. She stopped struggling.

"This is my final gift to you."

As Carol's body lay facedown, motionless, lifeless in his bunk, he removed the scarf and folded it neatly and respectfully placed it in the passenger's seat in the cab. He grabbed the folding chair from under the bunk and set it up just next to the truck. He began to eat the sandwiches he and Carol got. Good, they were still warm. The family business always gave him a strong appetite. Good thing he had two biscuits to enjoy this morning.

He needed to dispose of the body shortly. That was one thing he always liked about the desert; there were endless places for body dumps, and nothing was ever found.

After he finished up, he climbed back into the rig. As the big diesel engine roared to life, he glanced down at his watch. Great, that only took an hour. He could clean this up and be back to the house by ten, right on time to give Kaylee a ring. He pulled out of the truck stop and headed down the highway to a deserted area. Parts of the desert didn't see traffic for hours.

He found a small patch of vegetation just two hundred yards from the highway where some vultures gathered. Must be a carcass of something there. "I bet those vultures would really enjoy the sweet meat I have for them." He picked up the limp body from his bunk and walked over to the bushes. As he got closer, a half-eaten cow came into view.

The birds squawked loudly as he approached, voicing their dislike of him interrupting their meal. "I don't mean to disturb, just thought you may enjoy this bit as well." He laid the body next to the cow, being careful to take off her clothes and jewelry. He rubbed some of the cow blood on her body and wiped his hands with her clothes. He gathered everything up and headed back to the truck. When he was less than halfway back to his truck, the vultures returned to their feast, wildly squawking at the newest tasty dish for them to dine on.

Settled in his truck, the engine roaring to life, he glanced over the desert towards the group of birds. Numerous more had joined in the feast, some flying off with pieces they had pulled off. He smiled. "The circle of life." He laughed as he pulled onto the road. One could always count on the birds of prey scattering the remains across miles of isolated sand. Within hours, there would be no trace of Carol or the cow left. Maybe later today he would return to check for himself. No need, the Universe had this completely under control.

A few hours later, Curtis was back at the rental house in Flagstaff. After taking a shower, he picked up the phone and called Kaylee's hotel.

"Good morning, this is Kaylee." Her tone was exceptionally cheery.

"Good morning, Kaylee. Seeing it's Sunday, I thought you may just want to take it easy and chill by the pool and enjoy the desert sun."

"That sounds wonderful. There is a rooftop pool here at the hotel."

"We could go there, or I have a pool at my rental house as well. Whichever you prefer."

"Let's meet at your house. It would be nice for it to just be us so that we could get to know each other better."

"Perfect. The address is 122 Prairie Street. See you in an hour or so?"

"Sounds good. See you then. Oh, and Curtis?" She paused for just a second. "I'm glad you called."

This girl was special. She was definitely someone who would go tat for tat with him. He was excited to see her, to chat with her, to try to unravel the mystery that was Kaylee Smith-Roberts and what led her path to cross with his own.

A short while later, a car pulled up in the driveway, and he rushed to the door. "Hope you didn't have any trouble finding it?" He called to Kaylee as she gathered her things from the trunk of her car.

"No, not at all. I asked for directions at the front desk." She headed up the walk.

Curtis smiled and gave her a quick peck on the cheek as they passed. "The pool's around back. We can head through the house. There's a room for you to change in as well."

"Such the gentleman. Are you sure you don't want me to strip down in the living room, maybe jump up on the coffee table as well? That is, if you still have those singles in your wallet that you didn't give the Hopi lady last evening," Kaylee said.

Curtis was about to speak when Kaylee quickly rescinded. "I'm kidding."

"Damn, and I was getting all excited. Who doesn't like a live show? Especially when it is the most beautiful girl in the world!"

"How about a raincheck? Right now, I would like a cold drink to go with the hot sun."

"Coming right up, my dear. The bedroom is down the hall." Curtis watched her saunter down the hallway towards the bedroom.

As she looked back over her shoulder and caught him as he watched her walk away, she blew him a kiss. "I'll be right back."

Curtis grabbed a bucket and filled it with ice and reached for the cold bottles of beer from the fridge. He opened several drawers as he looked for the bottle opener.

"Ready?" The sweet voice came from behind him, her arms wrapped around his waist.

He turned in her arms. "I was born ready, babe." He looked into her eyes.

She raised her chin, her mouth slightly open.

He resisted, as he knew if he started he wouldn't be able to stop. He exhaled and bent down and met her lips softly with his. He lingered just a moment before he swatted her butt. "What do you say we go cool off in the pool? I think we both would benefit from a cold shower right about now."

"I could go for one of those cold beers." She quickly kissed him, grabbed a beer from the bucket, and headed for the back door.

Curtis picked up the bucket and followed her outside.

After several hours of swimming, sunning, and snacking, Curtis and Kaylee stretched out on the lounges by the pool. Kaylee asked about Curtis's childhood and what it was like growing up in North Carolina. "If you were writing your story of what made you who you are today, what would you write?"

"You are the writer, not me," Curtis said as he avoided her request.

"Okay, fair enough. Tell me about your mother. You talk about her a lot. You must be really close?"

"We were. Mom passed away just before I graduated high school." He lowered his head before taking a long swig of his beer.

"Oh, Curtis. I am so sorry. I didn't know," Kaylee reached over and squeezed his arm to comfort him.

"How would you know?" he responded as he looked at her and touched her hand. "We had a great bond. We still do. She is with me every day, just in a different way." He motioned towards the sky.

"I agree. People important to us never leave, even when they pass on." Skillfully, she changed the subject. "So what kind of kid were you in high school? I bet you were the star of the football team!"

"As a matter of fact, I was. I was the quarterback for the Fighting Bengals, and I was the pitcher for the baseball team as well."

"I bet you were very popular with the ladies." She reached over and ran her fingers through his dark, wet hair.

"I was rarely alone, if that's what you mean. I had a steady girlfriend through most of high school. Susan lived on the next farm. Her daddy had a cattle farm like mine, but he held the prestigious title of President of the North Carolina Cattlemen's Association." He remembered the jealousy his father had over not being named president. He paused, secretly rejoicing in the memory of his father's pain.

Kaylee noticed the edge of Curtis's mouth curl up slightly as she added, "Wow! He must have been a powerful man."

"He was important to many." He took a sip from his beer. "My father hated the fact that I spent more time with Susan and her family than with him. My father was a very selfish man. My mom certainly deserved better."

His words hung in the air. The cold beer mixed with the bitter memories of his dad made Curtis want to open up to Kaylee. Was that the right thing to do? As he finished that beer and reached for another, he began to speak again.

"Susan and I had a lot in common. Both our dads were on the road a lot, and this left our moms at home tending the farm and raising the family alone. They were both strong women. Susan's mom, Holly, was an adjunct professor at the local university about forty minutes away from their farm."

"That's quite impressive. I guess Susan was pretty smart as well?"

"She planned to follow in her mom's footsteps and work in the medical field but as a psychiatrist. Susan was fascinated with how human thought processes worked. She loved to explore how a person's environment shaped and molded them into who they became in life." His speech quickened as he sat up from the lounge chair and swung his legs over, facing Kaylee. "She lived to assess how random circumstances caused people's synapses to misfire, allowing their dark sides to comes out. Her passion was all about figuring out that exact moment, the trigger where their brain was rewired into a monster. Understanding that moment, she believed, would hold the answer to curing them."

"What do you think?"

His head tilted to the side as he studied her face. "I was always more interested in that moment that broke them. When they slipped up. How they got caught. Wasn't as interested in what made them the monsters."

Kaylee gazed into his eyes as his words hung in the air. Curtis realized at that moment that Kaylee truly "got" him. She didn't judge the way others had. He wanted to share everything with her. He longed to unload the burden he carried about his mom's death. Years of guilt, regret, rage. But could he really lower the mask? If she saw his demons, would she still not judge? How could anyone not loathe something so vile? It was his cross to bear, and one that he needed to carry alone.

"Why don't we see what kind of food we can scrounge up? I picked up some steaks that we can throw on the grill."

"That sounds great!"

As they puttered around in the kitchen, Kaylee coyly brought the conversation back to the relationship between Curtis and his mom. "Some of my happiest memories are when my grandma, my mom, and I were in the kitchen. I always loved to watch them cook and listen to the conversations and wild plans they talked about."

"I spent a lot more time with my grandpa, Pappy, where the wild plans were hatched. But I agree, some of my happiest memories, too, involve meals with my family at my grandparents' house in the Tennessee mountains."

"Those hours spent with those ladies made me who I am today. What about you, Curtis? Was Pappy the greatest influence on you?"

He thought for a moment. "Pappy definitely imprinted on me." He smiled. "But Mom is the single greatest influence in my life. We would often wake up early to watch the sunrise. Sometimes we talked, and sometimes we just sat."

"That is such a great memory. What was it about dawn that meant so much to you and your mother?" Kaylee nudged him as she seasoned the steaks.

"It is peaceful, calm, pure. The start of a new beginning. The first rays of sunshine peeking out from the horizon. Innocent, you know?"

"It certainly is. The dawning of a second chance, if you will. Signifying rebirth in a way." Kaylee expanded on Curtis's thoughts as she placed the steaks on the plate and went to wash her hands.

"I've had many 'new beginnings' in my life. Seemed as if I was always reinventing, reimagining, and restarting." He picked up the plate of steaks and headed to the grill. "One day in particular sticks out. It was just a few months before my high school graduation, and I had just spent the weekend at the beach with my girlfriend. I became a man that day."

Kaylee interrupted his story. "The day you lost your virginity?" She rubbed her hands together as she followed him out to the grill.

"Oh no. Not in the carnal sense. That was when I was fifteen. But that's a story for another day." He snickered at the memory. "This was a time that I was forced to grow up. The day I looked in the mirror and realized who I was and what I was to become. I knew at that very moment I didn't want to be like my father."

They both stood silently and stared out at the mountains, the sky, the universe as the steaks sizzled on the grill. Curtis sighed. "Sometimes your greatest teachers teach you what you don't want to be and thus help you become who you should."

Kaylee looked over at him as he turned towards her. "So true."

They both stared at each other for a moment longer before Curtis said, "It is so easy to talk to you. You are like an extension of me. How can that be as we just met?"

"Or maybe we have known each other forever. In our dreams. In our souls," Kaylee whispered, her eyes lowered to break eye contact before she looked back up at Curtis.

He told her about going to Smith High School, where he played both football and baseball and was an honor student with a 4.0 GPA. He had everything going for him. He was accepted at Duke University for the fall and had his beautiful girlfriend, Susan, and everything appeared to be working out for him.

"Ooohh, so is Susan who popped your cherry?" Kaylee giggled.

"No!" Curtis snapped. "I told you I wasn't going to talk about that story right now."

"Okay, sorry. I didn't mean to pry. So what did you and Susan talk about?"

"Kaylee, why would you want to hear about my past relationships? Susan and I are friends but will never be more. She is not what I need for a long-term life partner. We have a lot of shared interests but in some ways are very incompatible."

"How so?" Kaylee's calm voice seemed to give Curtis permission to share his darkest secrets.

Curtis prided himself on always being two or more steps ahead. That was why he never got caught. He explained what they would talk about and didn't answer Kaylee's question, knowing she would never call him on it. She was trying to build trust, lull him into a false sense of safety, gaining respect through empathy. He knew it well. After all, he was a charismatic killer.

With his signature eyebrow wink, he continued. "We would spend hours, sitting by the old oak tree next to the secret drop spot for the local shiners, talking and analyzing notorious killers: David Berkowitz (the Son of Sam), John Wayne Gacy (the Killer Clown), people like that. What made them tick, what was that moment that broke them. Serial killers only become truly famous once they get caught. That part always fascinated me. How did they slip up? Was it truly unplanned, or did they finally have enough and allow it to happen? Deep down, Susan always wondered why I was fixated on the end game."

Curtis could see that thoughts churned wildly in her head. He needed a distraction in case he said too much. "We used to go to Tennessee to visit my maternal grandparents. I always loved hanging out at the family farm and playing cards with Pappy and his friends. They made moonshine as a hobby, and we loved to just spend weekends with them. Pappy always had stories to tell. I am very close to them, especially since my mother's passing."

"And she was so young. Was she sick long?"

"Mom died of a broken heart. I don't wish that kind of pain on anyone. If I could rid the world of that, I would in a heartbeat."

"Tell me more about your mother."

"She was the best. When I would turn into the gravel driveway that led to our house, I would slow down so the rocks wouldn't ding up the paint on my car. I can still hear Mom's voice saying, 'Curtis, sometimes I think you love that car more than your own mother!' But nothing could be further from the truth. She always has a special place in my heart. She was always the first one I looked for in the stands at my games. I don't remember a time she wasn't there, cheering me on. She was the type of woman who always put others before herself. I always wished I would feel that kind of compassion for others. But alas, I seemed to inherit my father's attitude towards others. 'Just suck it up,' Dad would say. 'Nothing good ever comes from complaining.'"

"I can tell from the son she raised that she sounds like a lovely woman. One I wish I was able to meet."

"I think she would have liked you as well. Just like I do." He rocked towards her and gave her a small bump with his shoulder. They both smiled and laughed.

"This is getting entirely too serious. I think the steaks are ready."

"They look perfect." Kaylee wrapped her arms around his waist.

After they finished dinner, they stretched out on the couch watching TV. As the silence grew deafening, Curtis finally spoke. "You know when I told you my mom died of a broken heart? Well, she actually took her own life because of an affair my father had. His mistress was pregnant, and Mom just couldn't take the humiliation of all that. The idea of Dad taking another woman was bad enough, but conceiving a child was just too much. I found her in her bathtub, surrounded by lit candles, family photos, her favorite incense still burning in a tub full of red water. It was frightful yet serene at the same time. Does that even make sense? How can something elicit diametrically opposed feelings simultaneously?"

Kaylee reached out and covered his hand with her own and gently squeezed it.

Reassured, he went on. "Regardless, I tried to save her, but it was too late. I called 911, and my dad came, but she was already gone. She was a strong, prideful woman who valued societal perceptions. I don't blame her for her decision. I do regret that I didn't act to save her from the heartbreak. I knew about my father's affairs through the years. I had seen him together with various women. I even walked in on him one time. I always kept it to myself. I believed him when he said, 'They mean nothing to me. Curtis, you are too young to understand the complexities of long-term relationships. Your mother doesn't need to know. It would break her if she found out.' He was right. It did break her. Maybe if I had confided in her, if I had the nerve to tell her I knew, that she was supported, I could have saved her from the heartache that ultimately took her life. I failed her as a son, as a man. I am not worthy of the love she showed me. I am not worthy." He just lowered his head.

"Curtis, you are absolutely worthy, and you did not fail her. I understand your guilt, but you realize it is not your fault your mother took her life. Even if you told her, that may not have resulted in her making a different choice. You can't change history. All we can do is continue to move forward, learn from it, make better choices."

"Exactly. From that point forward, I realized what my purpose in life was. What my legacy would be. How I would make a difference. I knew that I would be the type of man who treated women with respect, who protected them from harm and heartache. I do it in my mother's honor, to honor her memory, to not let her death and life be in vain. To show her and the world that her commitment to family lived on in me and I have the ability to impact others in such a way that they will not have to experience pain from relationships."

"Curtis, that is beautiful. I feel the love you have for her and for all people. I admire your dedication and commitment. I can see that you truly care about others, and that is what attracts me to you."

He raised his eyes to hers, searching for her truth. Could this really be? Could a woman truly find him attractive from an emotional sense and not just physical? Could this creature sitting beside him truly care for him? Was he worthy of love? He wanted to believe that she was different, that she would accept him even if she saw behind the mask. He decided to remove it for just a moment and see what her reaction would be.

As they laid on the couch wrapped in each other's arms, he broke the silence. "I found my dad and one of his mistresses in my parents' bed one Sunday when I arrived home early from a camping trip with my buddies. I don't think Dad ever realized that I saw them. When I was heading to my room, I heard noise coming from my parents' room. For some reason I decided to go check it out. There was a strange car in the drive, and I knew that Mom wasn't expected back for two more days.

"I think I knew what I would find behind their door before I opened it. I dreaded it, but at the same time, I needed to know for sure. I walked towards the door;

it was slightly ajar. I could hear the moans get louder as I got closer. But I had to find out the truth. I gently pushed open the door until I could clearly see them. This blonde woman was in my parents' bed, and she was tied up with several of my mother's scarves, including having one tied in a gag over her mouth. That is why the noises sounded muffled and strained.

"It was bad enough that my father was having sex with his mistress in the house, even in their bed, but the fact that he was living out his bondage fantasy using Mom's favorite scarves was unbelievable. At that moment I realized he had no respect for her at all. I always knew my parents' marriage was not the best, and they used to always say, 'We stay together separately.' I think I finally understand what that meant."

"Curtis, no one should have to shoulder that kind of burden, let alone a child. Your father was wrong. And you are right, your mother deserved better."

"You see, that woman I saw that day, she was the one that ended up pregnant. That ultimately was the final straw that broke my mother. And I kept seeing it in my mind as I sat with my mom, holding her wrists, wrapping them in the very scarves that Dad had put on that woman for his own pleasure. I tell you I wanted to kill them both. I felt justified in doing it as well. The pain that they inflicted in Mom's life, in my life. They deserved to suffer the same fate."

"I'm sure that the fact that your father used something so personal as your mother's scarves to fulfill his sexual fantasies was like putting salt on a wound."

For a split second, Curtis panicked and thought he had said too much. She couldn't know about the scarves. How could she? He was very careful. None of the missing women reports had mentioned anything about a scarf. His paranoia was starting to play tricks with his mind. Curtis quickly squelched his fears. He convinced himself she knew nothing of the scarves. "The whole thing was hard to witness. No one thing stood out." He was happy with his response. He handled it well, and she certainly didn't pick up on anything. Women always wanted to believe everyone had positive intent. Or did they?

"I'm glad you shared that with me. I know how hard it was for you. Thank you for trusting me."

As she drove back to her hotel, her mind kept replaying the day's events in her head. As the narratives replayed, Kaylee kept thinking she should be shocked. Any normal person would have a strong reaction to what Curtis shared. Except Kaylee didn't. She shared Curtis's view. What did that say about her? What did that say about them? Why would she find this reaction justified? The thought of truly knowing the answers scared her. She pushed her thoughts aside and focused on Curtis. What were the clues, the breadcrumbs in this tale? She realized he mentioned his mother's scarves. Could there be a link to the missing women? It was a long shot, but it also served as just the distraction Kaylee was looking for so that she could stop thinking about her own responses.

Curtis's reaction had not gone unnoticed by Kaylee. She had made a career based on detection of the smallest response in people. Her criminal justice degree perfected her sense of observation. That initial split-second reaction, the one that appeared when the shroud of secrecy lowered and a glimpse into the true persona is revealed. She saw it. She saw the true Curtis, and surprisingly, she was intrigued. She realized at that very moment this man before her was the one she had longed for. The nameless face in those hazy visions that haunted her through the years. He was the one, her destiny. Did he feel the same?

Kaylee knew in her gut that there was more to Curtis than appeared at first glance. For now, she was content with allowing him to think she didn't notice. After all, if he really was a killer, she certainly didn't want to get on his bad side.

~ CHAPTER 9 ~

THE MASONS

Curtis and Kaylee enjoyed the next few days together in Flagstaff before they parted ways. They agreed they would stay in contact once they got back to their normal lives. As Curtis drove his truck back to North Carolina, he decided to take a little detour and see Pappy in Tennessee. Curtis parked his rig on the side of the road in front of his grandparents' house. As he walked up the drive, Tucker's barking announced his arrival.

Grandma wiped her hands on a towel as she walked out on the front porch, most likely because she was in the kitchen creating a wonderful meal. "Curtis, what a pleasant surprise. We weren't expecting you."

"No, Grandma. I was just on my way back from Flagstaff and decided to stop in and see you guys."

Hugging Grandma, he got a whiff of cookies baking. "You must have sensed I was on my way and made my favorite thing: your chocolate chip cookies!"

"Must have. I just had an inkling to whip up a batch. Your timing was impeccable. Come on in, and I'll get 'em on a plate for you. Pappy is out in the shed as usual. I know he will be tickled to see you."

Curtis grabbed a few warm cookies from the plate and headed out the back door towards the shed. He shoved the last bite of cookie in his mouth when Pappy saw him coming. "Curtis, aren't you a sight for sore eyes. How ya doing?" He gave his grandson a big hug. "And you didn't even bring me a cookie? I guess I'll have to let that slide this time. As long as there are some left when we get back in."

"There will be. Grandma just pulled out the first sheet. Her cookies are legendary."

Pappy showed Curtis what he was working on in the shed. "I'm just out here tinkering with this old tractor engine. Seems to be making a bit of noise lately. Just have to give it a good cleaning and sprucing. So what have you been up to?"

Curtis hesitated a little. "I was just out in Arizona. Spent a few days bumming around. Went to Winslow and toured the Hopi ruins. It was very interesting how they lived and how they related to the spirit worlds. We even had dinner at the La Mesa Familiar."

"I love that place. First big hotel on the railroad out there. Grandma and I have stayed there several times. You said 'we.' Did you meet a friend out there?"

"You could say that. Her name is Kaylee. I met her in Winslow. She was standing on a corner, and we started chatting."

Pappy looked up at him and smiled. "She must be something very special to have my grandson so flustered."

"I'm not flustered!" Curtis insisted. "We just had a really great time."

Pappy nodded his head as he winked at Curtis. "Sure thing, Curtis. So help me with these spark plugs, and we can run inside and get some more cookies." Pappy expertly redirected the conversation.

After they finished with the tractor, they headed inside and got cleaned up. As Curtis headed back from the washroom, he overheard Pappy. "Curtis has found a love interest. Apparently, they met in Arizona on his trip, and she seems to have captured our little man's attention. He seems quite smitten from what I see."

"Don't you pressure that young man," Grandma cautioned. "He is still young and may not be ready to settle down and get serious with anyone."

Pappy just smiled as if he knew this lady was different. How did he do that? He hadn't even met her, but he knew. Curtis shook his head.

As the sun started to set, Curtis and Pappy headed out to the firepit with a jar of Pappy's latest mountain elixir. Stretched out in the chairs, Pappy started to speak. "Curtis, it's been a while since we have had a chance to chat. You know, I can remember way back when I first met your grandmother. I knew immediately she was different. She made me question how long I wanted to continue my bachelor ways."

Pappy could tell he needed advice and, as usual, knew exactly what the topic was before Curtis even said it. "Pappy. She is different. Kaylee is a journalist from Chicago. She was in Flagstaff doing research for a story she is writing. She had the most striking green eyes. They pierce your soul when she looks at you. She is so smart and really into culture and history. We talked for hours about everything and nothing. It seemed like she just 'got me,' if you know what I mean."

"Oh do I. That kind of connection is rare, that's for sure. Especially for us. You know when someone comes into our lives and we feel safe enough to let down our guard and allow them to see behind the curtain, so to speak, they are special indeed. This lady, Kaylee, is she like that?"

"I think so, Pappy. That's why I'm here."

"I figured." Pappy took a sip from the mason jar.

"The rules are there for a reason. To protect us. To protect you. You have to be thoughtful in who you allow into the circle."

"I know. How did you know to let Grandma into the circle?"

Sitting up straighter in his chair, whispering so no one would hear. "Curtis, Grandma knows nothing and never will. She would not understand. The guilt would be more than she could bear. Thus, she never can know."

Curtis noticed the sternness in his voice. But how could Pappy have kept it a secret for all these years? He didn't even have to ask the question before Pappy went on to explain.

"As we have talked about in the past, you have to compartmentalize parts of your life. It's a mechanism to protect you and everyone around you. You have given in to your taste for blood and with that comes responsibilities. It's the cross you must bear. Sometimes you will have to bear it alone, other times you have someone that will help shoulder the load. It has been a solo adventure for me after Great-grandpappy passed away so many years ago, until you. It hasn't always been easy, and my love of hunting has helped curb my desires a bit. But there is nothing like the thrill of chasing the most cunning prey there is: humans." That spark in Pappy's eye was one that Curtis knew well. He had seen it many times over the years. From their talks about serial killers with Susan to the night at the firepit when Curtis found out he wasn't alone.

Pappy refocused. "But you know that already." He chuckled. "Curtis, only you truly know if she is worthy."

Curtis responded, "Pappy, I am not sure, but I think she may be one of us. I just don't know how to tell."

"Ummm. That's a hard one, son. What makes you think that?"

"Well, she is very interested in killers, she draws inferences and connections that few others would, and she isn't scared when—" He cut himself off, hesitating to confide in Pappy that he had told her about the scarves and how he wanted to kill Dad and Candice. At least he didn't spill everything.

"Curtis, you didn't?"

"No, I didn't tell her. But we talked about Mom and her death. And I mentioned Dad and seeing him with Candice and the scarves."

"Oh, Curtis." Pappy shook his head. "No wonder you showed up here. You have been diligent about the rules, and other than the scarves, there is no link between your victims. And most people won't even know they wore scarves in their final moments. She probably doesn't even know. You said she was a journalist, right? Conducting research? What was the topic?"

"She was there for, ummm…" He realized he didn't know what she was researching. Going back through their conversations, she really didn't talk about herself very much at all. She had a way of making him feel comfortable, and he let his guard down. He lowered his mask just a bit. Gave slight glimpses at the man behind the mask. "You know, Pappy, I don't know. We seemed to talk more about me than her."

Pappy scratched his forehead the way he did when he was pondering difficult situations. "That could prove problematic. Yes, it could. But I've been here before. No need to panic. We just have to figure this one out. Do you think you will see her again?"

"Without a doubt, Pappy! Without a doubt!"

"Well then, perhaps she may enjoy a nice home-cooked meal in eastern Tennessee?"

"I think she would very much. That way you can meet her, too, and we can go from there. Pappy?" He lowered his voice. "I really like her."

"I know you do. We just have to figure out how to incorporate her into the family, if you will. Is she like Grandma or something else? We will figure it out."

He felt better. He knew that Pappy had his back and would never intentionally steer him wrong. Now at least they had a plan. He was glad he had Pappy to confide in.

Curtis arrived at the airport to see the girl who would change his life. He stood at the meeting spot with a bouquet of flowers and a big smile on his face. He anxiously scanned the crowds coming through the gateway from the arriving planes. He wiped the moisture from his hands onto his jeans, shifting back and forth on his feet. Her plane landed twenty minutes ago; she should be here soon.

He then caught a glimpse of her, the long dark hair, striking green eyes; she looked more beautiful than he remembered. They had talked almost daily since they had left Flagstaff almost two months before. He was so excited to see her again and show her his life in North Carolina. He had arranged to have the week off, so they had plenty of time to sit back on the farm, check out the local hot spots, and even head to Tennessee to see his grandparents.

As she got closer and finally saw Curtis, she started to run. Kaylee jumped into his arms and kissed him passionately. "Hi stranger," she said when they came up for air.

"You look great!" He stepped back, and his eyes took in every inch of her. "These are for you. Pretty flowers for a pretty lady."

"Thank you so much! They are beautiful! Let's go get my bag so we can get out of here and say a proper hello." His eyebrows raised as he winked and took her hand and led the way to baggage claim.

A few minutes later, they headed down the highway towards the ranch. Kaylee didn't know a lot about where Curtis lived. He hoped she wouldn't feel overwhelmed. The presence of the plantation house sometimes took some getting used to. But she was from Chicago. There was a lot of old money there too.

As they approached the farm, the old stone fence came into view. Kaylee commented on how she always loved the old fieldstone walls in the South by the old houses and farms. Curtis smiled; she would love and appreciate the MacIntyre farm. As they approached the large iron gate that marked the drive, flanked by the two tall stone pillars, Curtis slowed the Mustang and pushed the button to open the huge gate. He glanced over at Kaylee and caught a look of surprise as she realized this was where they were going.

"Welcome home, Kaylee. This is me."

"Damn, Curtis! Why didn't you tell me you were fucking rich?"

"My parents built the farm and business; I just inherited it and run it as a silent partner. I'm not involved in the day-to-day cattle operations much anymore. I couldn't move out of my family home. My mother loved this house, and it means a lot to me as well."

"I can see why. It is like a castle. The stonework is amazing. And the front portico, that is breathtaking. This would be a magnificent place for a wedding. The flowers, the house, the rolling fields." Kaylee cut herself off. "Sorry about that, I was just getting excited. I'm not looking to marry a rich guy or anything like that."

He laughed. "You came here before you knew where I lived. I know you are not a gold digger. Let's get your stuff inside, and I can show you around."

She willingly jumped out of the car when he pulled up to the front circle. "And to think I was excited about riding in the Mustang down the country roads. Boy, I sure undershot on the expectations." They both laughed as he grabbed her suitcase out of the trunk and carried it up the large stone steps to the carved wooden doors. "Your palace awaits, my lady." He gestured her into the front hall.

She just looked around in awe. He tried to see it through her eyes. From the marble floors to the carved balusters and the newel post and the oriental carpets on the floor. This house was a museum. "This is the front hall with the office and living room to the right and left. The center hall runs back to the kitchen and great room. There are halls on either side that go to the east and west wings. There is a library, billiard room to the left and the gym and garage is off to the right. We can head upstairs, and I can show you the guest rooms. You can pick which you would like."

"I thought I would be staying with you in your room."

"Sure, but I didn't want to presume. But that is what I was hoping. Let me show you the way." He headed off towards the main staircase. Once they got upstairs, he explained that after Mom passed away and Dad met with that terrible accident with the grinder out in the barn, he completely remodeled the entire upstairs. His suite was in the east wing as he liked the morning sun to come in his windows. They made their way down the hall past three bedrooms before they reached the massive double doors to the owner's suite.

"How big is this house?"

"It is fifteen thousand square feet, give or take. Nine bedrooms and twelve baths. There is a ballroom on the third floor, too, and a swimming pool in the basement."

"Do you have a torture chamber or dungeon too?" Kaylee asked as she crossed her wrists and raised her arms over her head as if she was restrained.

"Well, Ms. Smith-Roberts, that could be arranged, if you so wanted." He opened the doors to the most magnificent bedroom she had ever seen. A huge four-post bed complete with steps on each side was placed against the far wall. A sitting area with bookshelves was at the end surrounded by windows overlooking the pastures.

The windows were floor to ceiling, and it looked like something out of a history book. "The baths are in the back, separate his and hers."

Kaylee looked at him a little bewildered.

"Some things I don't like to share. Do you want to make yourself at home and unpack?"

"Maybe we can just check out this bed for a bit." She jumped over the end, landing in the pile of pillows. "I can't believe you actually live here. You drive a truck for Christ sake. Most truck drivers don't live like this."

"I enjoy traveling and driving the truck. It gives me a chance to just be me and not have all this baggage. No one knows I'm that rich MacIntyre kid whose mom killed herself when his father knocked up his mistress. Sometimes it's nice to just be Curtis the Truck Driver."

"I get it. Many people recognize my name from the articles and publications I have. They don't recognize my face, but when they hear my name they will ask, 'Did you write this?' They either love or hate it, and they don't hesitate to tell you just what they think. Sometimes I like to go unnoticed as well."

"I was thinking while you are here, it may be fun to take a drive out to Tennessee. We can see my grandparents, and you can sample our family's moonshine and Grandma's fabulous cooking."

"That would be wonderful," she answered without hesitation. "But for now, maybe we can hang here and get reacquainted."

Early the next morning, Curtis and Kaylee packed the car and headed out towards the east Tennessee mountains. It was a long drive, but they never lacked for conversation. As the landscape changed and the gently rolling hills turned steeper and higher, the soft peaks of the Smoky Mountains came into view in the distance. The air turned cooler, and the humidity dropped. "Wow, you can really feel the change in temperature as you get in the mountains," Kaylee said.

"Oh yes. It's ten to fifteen degrees cooler up here. We should be at Pappy's in a few hours if you want to rest a bit before we get there. It was an early start this morning."

That was a good idea. She reclined the Mustang's seat back and closed her eyes. She felt so safe with Curtis. She never felt like this with others. It was hard to believe he could be a killer, she thought as she drifted off to sleep.

Several hours later, they pulled into the driveway, and Curtis rubbed her arm softly. "We are here, babe."

Looking out the window, they were greeted by a cute little country farmhouse with a wide porch, rocking chairs, and a porch swing. A brown dog's bark announced their arrival. An older man with white hair and a lady with a summer dress and apron on came onto the porch, the wooden screen door slammed shut behind them.

"Curtis, you made it," the man said as they got out of the car. He approached the car, hand extended. "Nice to meet you, pretty lady. You must be Kaylee. I am Darryl Mason, Curtis's grandpappy, and this is Martha, my wife and Curtis's grandma. Curtis has told us about you, and it is certainly our pleasure to host you in our home."

"Come on in, dear. I'm sure you are thirsty after that long ride from Carolina. Let me get you a glass of cold iced tea." Grandma headed back to the kitchen.

Kaylee graciously followed her. "You have such a lovely home. So inviting, and I just love the front porch and the flower boxes."

"Why thank you, my dear. I do love my flowers. Our late daughter, Debra, loved gardening as well. It was something we always enjoyed together. She planted so many flowers here growing up, and she did a wonderful job on the gardens at the plantation house. Did you see that already?"

"I did. The grounds were lovely. It was like a park. I didn't realize your daughter had designed all the gardens there. That is quite the tribute. She was very talented."

"That she was. Curtis doesn't have the same passion for the gardens as his mother did. But he loves that house. And there is a lot of her still there as well. Her death has been hard on him. He struggled to find his way for a while. And I'm not sure he really has yet. But I can say his eyes lit up when he spoke about you. And I can see why."

Heat danced across Kaylee's face. "Well, Curtis and I had a good time in Arizona, and I'm glad I got the chance to see him again and to meet you both as well."

Curtis and Pappy walked in and sat in the living room. "Well, the bags are all up in the guest rooms. You both should be all comfy in there. I see Grandma got you some tea already. Hopefully you ladies enjoyed a little henpecking."

"Oh, Darryl!" Grandma scolded. "We were just admiring the flowers and talking about Debra's gardens back at the plantation house."

Curtis saw the confused looked on Kaylee's face and explained, "Henpecking is how Pappy refers to women's banter."

Kaylee nodded as she sipped the tea.

"Do you like gardening, Kaylee?" Pappy asked.

"I love flowers, but being in the city of Chicago with only a small balcony, I can't have a lot of plants myself. But I do enjoy walking through various botanical gardens in Chicago and other cities. I hope one day when I move out of the city, I can have big gardens of my own."

"That would be nice, wouldn't it?" Grandma added. "We definitely have enjoyed our space. We have always been country folk. But I do appreciate a trip into the city, just don't want to live there full time."

"Each has their pros and cons. I can appreciate both as well." Kaylee took a sip of her iced tea. "I've never been to the Smoky Mountains before. I'm sure there are a lot of stories in these hills."

Pappy raised his eyebrow and glanced at Curtis. "Yes, there are many stories in these hills, little lady. All fit for telling, some not in mixed company, I'm afraid. The family ties here run deep; the rocks hold a lot of secrets. We've been on this mountain for over one hundred years. I was born here, and this is where I will die as well. Lots has changed over the years, but again, a lot has remained. I'm glad Curtis likes to come up here and see us. It's good to be able to share your history with the next generation. I hope one day he will bring his family here too."

"I can tell that family is important to Curtis. The way he speaks of you both, his mother, the farm, his family. It is evident. He is a great man, very respectful, honest, and caring. That's something I noticed right away."

Curtis blushed now. "Kaylee, really, you don't need to say all that."

"But it's true. You are a kind, loving person, and that makes me feel safe."

"And that's important, to feel safe, Kaylee." Pappy picked up his tea and took a sip.

Kaylee helped Grandma fix dinner as Pappy and Curtis headed out to the shed.

After they enjoyed a sumptuous dinner, Pappy suggested they head out to enjoy the night sky around the fire. Grandma gladly shooed them outside as she tidied up and started dessert. "I have my legendary chocolate lava cakes with ice cream. I'll just have to pop them in the oven for about thirty minutes or so. Kaylee, why don't you join the boys outside? I'm sure Darryl would love to be able to spend some time getting to know you better."

Curtis, Kaylee, and Pappy gathered around the small, crackling fire Curtis expertly built. "We've spent many nights out here, me and Pappy. Solving our world's problems. From small things to life-and-death issues. No topic is off limits for us. Pappy is a great listener and gives pretty good advice as well," Curtis stated. "He had never steered me wrong, anyway."

"Curtis, thank you so much, my boy. I enjoy the time spent with family, young and old. It's what is truly important in life. At the end of the day, family are the ones you can count on when the chips are down. They always have your back. Or at least they should." Pappy sat back in his chair as the flames flickered in the night sky.

Kaylee smiled. She loved the relationship Curtis had with his grandparents. It was nice to see that connection. Curtis had suffered a lot of loss in his life. He struggled with trust and had built a wall. He obviously had a lot of past relationships but not a whole lot of serious ones. How many of his women had Pappy met over the years?

Pappy was the key to unlocking Curtis's secret, she knew that. She just wasn't sure if she was ready to open that door yet. In fact, she knew that she didn't want to do it face-to-face. "So Pappy," Kaylee started, "tell me about Curtis when he was younger. What was he like growing up?"

"What you see is what you get with Curtis. He's a good guy, was a very smart student, was bound for Duke when his mother passed. He played lots of sports too. Excels at most everything he tries. Curtis likes to be recognized." Pappy leaned over, patting him on his shoulder. "I think secretly he wanted to be famous, even as a young boy. Had to catch the biggest fish." Pappy pretended to cast a fishing pole and reel in a big fish. "I can tell you about one time, with his first girlfriend, Susan. They were in kindergarten, that was long before they were dating, but they grew up down the road from each other and her father was a cattleman, too, like Curtis's dad, so the families socialized on several fronts."

Kaylee recognized the reference to his high school girlfriend. She must have played a key role in his life on several levels. "I would love to hear an embarrassing story about little Curtis." She laughed.

Curtis shook his head and sat back to listen to a story that was clearly familiar.

"Anyway, Curtis here decided he wanted to enter the science fair at the elementary school. He was six years

171

old, and little Susan and he played daily, so of course they both decided they would enter projects. Curtis built a battery pack that powered a headlight on his bicycle by taking energy from the back wheel when it spins. And Susan, she grew a bunch of different types of crystals, if I remember correctly." He scratched his head. "So they both created these very elaborate displays with demonstrations, diagrams. Curtis had his bike there on a stand so people could jump on and pedal fast to light the lamp. Susan had rock candy that she grew for people to eat."

"Anyhoo, we all came and walked through the fair, and Curtis and Susan both proudly told everyone about their projects and why they should win. At the end of the evening, they got around to announcing the winners. They called out the first, second, and third places for the fifth graders and then the fourth and third grades. Then the second and first grades. Curtis was getting really excited because he knew the kindergarteners were coming up. Then they just called all of them up to the stage and handed them all a participation ribbon."

"Curtis graciously accepted his ribbon, just as his mother would expect. It was yellow, and the disappointment shone on his face as he fussed with that ribbon. Curtis came over to where we were all gathered and he said, 'When are they going to announce who won first place? Who got the blue ribbon?' His momma looked down at Curtis and said, 'Oh Curtis, honey, I don't think they give that to the kindergarteners. You all are winners. But you got a really nice ribbon and certificate. I bet we can have a really nice frame made for it and hang it in the library so everyone will see it.' Curtis just looked at his yellow ribbon and said, 'Well, yeah, that would be nice, but Momma? I really wanted the blue ribbon. If you can't get first place, why bother to enter at all? Someone needs to win, and someone needs to not win. That's the way it is!' he said."

Kaylee and Curtis laughed.

"Okay, so you know my secret. I learned at an early age to only enter science fairs where you can win blue ribbons."

"That's a great story. I like it, Pappy. I think it sums up Curtis quite nicely, in fact."

"How so?" Pappy leaned back in his chair as he took a long sip of his drink. "I'd like to hear your take on my grandson and his motivations."

"Since you asked," she glanced over at Curtis, "I think there are many sides to him. I think he is most likely a Gemini. He has his competitive side, and that competitive side shows up quite often. It's the side that drives him and motivates him to be the best. He loves to be recognized, but it must be for something he has accomplished and earned. He doesn't like to be recognized due to his family name or their public life. His confidence comes from within, and he is intrinsically motivated. He has a softer side as well. He doesn't trust naturally. You have to earn your place with Curtis, be let into his inner circle. Once you are there, though, I think what you find might be a little surprising, perhaps even, one may say, a bit shocking."

"Shocking!" Curtis interrupted loudly. "Why would you say shocking?"

"I met you in Winslow, and we spent days together, ate at a nice restaurant, talked for hours. You never mentioned that you lived in a gigantic palace or that you were a millionaire truck driver. You suffered a traumatic loss of your mother at a young age, and that changes your relationships with people going forward. I think some of your history, your story, can be a bit shocking, a bit unexpected."

"I think you are quite perceptive. And although apparently Curtis doesn't agree, I can see how our family history can come across to outsiders as surprising. It certainly is not the norm. But we aren't a normal kind of bunch." Pappy gave a little laugh.

"You certainly are not. But I don't think I would be attracted to 'normal.' It can be rather boring, if I do say so. Curtis is outgoing and charismatic. Extremely attractive, cultured, and very intelligent. He is one of a kind."

"So, Curtis, what do you have to say for yourself, young man? You've obviously stolen this young lady's heart."

"Shit, I don't know." He put on a strong Southern accent. "I'm not all that cultured. I'm just a country boy at heart." They all laughed. He took a more serious tone. "But honestly, I really do like you, Kaylee, and you know that it's mutual or you wouldn't be here. Pappy and Grandma are like my parents, and I respect their opinion. Although I haven't asked, I think they approve as well. I think there is only one more test that you need to pass."

She and Pappy looked towards Curtis, a little bewildered. "Pappy, you have any mash we can run? Kaylee here needs to show us she can run with the big boys."

"I'm sure I can round some up. Let's head on up to the back shed and see."

The three of them walked to the shed that housed the old copper still. Kaylee had never made moonshine before and honestly hadn't ever tasted it either, but she was ready to tackle anything. Pappy and Curtis explained everything to her in as much detail as she needed. They were very patient, as being a reporter, she always asked a lot of questions. Soon they had the fire heating up under the pot and were ready to start. After a bit of time, the more volatile alcohols, those with the lowest boiling points, the heads, started coming out the other end, and Pappy and Curtis showed her how to tell from the smell when the ethanol was starting to come off. Acetaldehyde first, followed by acetone, esters and methanol, then the ethanol, the heart or spirit you want to collect, and finally the alcohols with high boiling points, like butyl alcohol, in the tails. It seems a little more of an art to get the cut right; you had to separate the heart from the head and tails.

After much sniffing, sipping, and spitting, the time had finally arrived. "Start catching!" Pappy exclaimed. The magical clear liquid dripped into jug after jug, and the two men moved in perfect harmony collecting, capping, sipping, and finally they declared that was a wrap. Deciding they would clean up later, Curtis grabbed a jug and poured some into a small mason jar he got from the shelf. "We'll take this up to the house. It should go perfectly with the lava cakes."

"This shine goes perfectly with everything!" Pappy stated.

Heading back to the house, Kaylee was beaming with pride. She had made her first illegal moonshine, in an old copper still, with a man she only met a few months ago, whom she barely knew but had somehow stolen her heart. He was the one for her, that she knew was true. But she also knew there was more to this boy than met the eye. She just wasn't sure how to figure it out, and if she did, would she still love this man? As they walked back to the house, she knew what she needed to do as she reached for Curtis's hand.

~ CHAPTER 10 ~

The Note

Curtis enjoyed his first weekend off in a while. After he spent a week with Kaylee, traveled to Tennessee, followed by ten straight days on the road, he was ready for a break. He pulled into the yard Friday afternoon, turned in his manifest, and parked his rig. He was ready to head back to the house and enjoy the peace and quiet of the country life.

The sun was high in the sky by the time he headed downstairs for his first cup of coffee of the day. Although he loved the time spent with Kaylee and his friends, he also really appreciated his alone time. This was the time where he could really recharge, reexamine, and reset.

His thoughts drifted back to how Kaylee had expertly managed the still, how she listened to their instructions, questioned and mastered the process like it was second nature to her. He could tell that Pappy was impressed as well.

Something still nagged at him though. She still had a secret, that he knew was true. He, too, had his secret; did she sense it? Did she realize what he and Pappy did in their spare time? That between them they had killed over two-hundred people, seventy-five for Curtis alone? There was no way she could know.

He and Pappy had done their homework. They knew she specialized in missing people. She reported on unsolved crimes. Sure there were missing women, but no one had linked any of their victims together. No one had realized that the body count for them alone spanned over sixty years. Curtis was more prolific than Pappy, but the first was only a decade prior. Curtis was twenty-eight, and his first kill was a few months shy of his eighteenth birthday. Pappy was much older, but his rate was much slower.

After he poured his second cup of coffee, he jumped in the golf cart and headed up the drive to the mailbox.

The mailman always came in the morning, so his trip wasn't unfruitful. A stack of magazines, advertising postcards, and a few letters greeted him as he opened the mailbox. One was hand addressed. Who would be sending him a personal letter? Perplexed, he turned it over and saw the return address was from I.C. You, 15-40 Main Street, Anytown, NC, USA. This intrigued Curtis.

Always ready for a little game of detective, he placed the mail on the seat beside him and looked around. He wasn't sure what he expected to find exactly, but perhaps someone who sent the letter might be close by. He didn't notice anything out of the ordinary. A couple of cars passed as he sat by the front gate. They all had North Carolina plates. He didn't recognize anyone, but that wasn't unusual either.

He would take a closer look at the letter inside. He stomped on the pedal, and the golf cart responded as it whizzed down the paved path winding through the trees towards the circle in front of the big house. He was almost giddy at the thought of what was inside. This was not going to be an ordinary, uneventful Saturday. This would be a fun way to spend the day, playing a real-life Clue game.

Sitting down at the round kitchen table, Curtis held the letter from I.C. You, turning it over as he inspected it from every angle. There was a stamp, and it was postmarked from an amusement park in Orlando, Florida. He laughed a little at that, as he always loved to buy postcards while their family visited the park and then mail them back to himself just to get the park postmark. Was that a clue? Did this person know that from his past? Was there something specific about the park?

He hesitated just a bit before opening the letter. A printed letter neatly folded in thirds rested inside the envelope. Pulling it out, he wondered if he should put on gloves. But then he laughed out loud. Why would he care about that? A serial killer didn't need to call the police to help him protect himself. Unfolding the letter, he began to read it. He quickly realized this would not be a good day.

Dear Curtis,

You like to play games? Well, I have a game for you.

The rules are simple, the clues are few.

The happiest place is not as it seems.

The cat and the mouse fight over the cheese.

The life that you see is not all that it seems.

The lie that you lead, is that all you can be?

I know who you are, but you don't know about me.

As time waxes on, I will be here

Waiting and counting and always quite near.

By the blue light of darkness, evils will stir

Searching and plotting to find the cure.

The only thing left is to seize the day

Before the hunter becomes the prey.

As you know well, no one gets out alive.

I can keep a secret and someone dies.

Maybe it was paranoia, maybe it was self-preservation. Either way, he understood what this note meant. Someone knew his secret, and this person was out for blood. He couldn't help but feel proud that another killer sought him out and challenged him like this.

The next few hours were consumed by analysis. What did it mean? He knew right away this was meant to be fun. He got the cat-and-mouse reference, but who was the cheese? Were the victims the cheese? Was a specific person the cheese? Was the game player planning to send more messages, more clues? Was he supposed to respond, and how could he respond? He didn't know who the person was. Excited and alarmed, Curtis knew he needed to play.

After a little research, he was able to decipher the reference to the full moon. There was a full moon August 2, 1993 and August 31, 1993. Since the August 31 full moon would be the second full moon of the month, it is referred to as a blue moon. So he had to do something by the 31st of August, but he wasn't quite sure what.

Searching and pondering, analyzing and dissecting for hours, he focused on the lines, "Seize the day/Before the hunter becomes the prey/As you know well, no one gets out alive/I can keep a secret and someone dies." He was the hunter that was now being stalked, but who was to die? Were they asking to team up with him and kill someone? Another killer perhaps? Somehow he needed to respond, but how? He thought about calling Pappy, but he wasn't ready for that yet. He had six weeks until the end of August. This would be a fun game of cat and mouse.

He figured out a way to send a message to the killer that he was ready to engage. What better way for serial killers to communicate but through their kills? He decided he would travel to the Kingsland amusement park in California on his next trip and select three ladies that were involved with cheese in some way—worked at a dairy or perhaps enjoying a cheese plate at a restaurant. He would figure that out when he got there. It needed to be three, a trifecta. He needed to show that he was not to be beat. He was the ultimate killer.

As he picked up his truck and headed out across Interstate 40, he arrived in Barstow, California, halfway between Las Vegas and LA. Barstow was a major transportation hub for the metropolitan area of Southern California. He was only 120 miles from LA, so while his rig was getting serviced and his trailer unloaded and reloaded, he hopped in a loaner car and headed west to the coast, to the crowning glory of Southern California, the land of kings. Curtis couldn't help but feel excited. Not only was he going to feed his thirst for blood today, he would send a strong message to his challenger that he was one to be reckoned with, that he was cunning and shrewd.

As he parked his car and headed to the entrance and passed under the archway, he wondered if he could pull this off. After all, he normally didn't work in crowded areas like this. But Curtis was nothing if not confident, so off he went to find his "cheese."

It didn't take him long to find a group of three ladies enjoying a glass of wine and some cheese under the shade of a few trees. He ordered a glass of Merlot and walked over to a nearby table and sat down. As he sipped his wine, he listened to their conversation when he overheard them encouraging one of the ladies to leave her abusive husband. This was just what he was waiting for. His next victim had arrived. He continued to listen before joining in at just the right moment. His charming demeanor always put the ladies at ease. This was going to be easier than he thought.

After chatting for a while and realizing that Curtis was all alone, they asked him to join them. He would round out their party nicely, as most of the rides were for two people. Curtis happily accepted, and off they went to enjoy the beautiful summertime weather in Southern California.

As the sun started to get low in the sky, they all were getting tired and agreed it was time to leave. As they exited the park, Curtis asked if they would like to enjoy one more glass of wine and cheese at a local shop he noticed just outside the park. Of course, the ladies jumped at the chance to accompany this exotic Adonis and enjoy another glass before they said goodbye.

The ladies piled into their car and blindly followed Curtis to the small wine shop and picked up a bottle of wine and a cheese plate to go. They headed to the park that one of the ladies suggested, as the view of the sunset was spectacular there.

As the ladies spread out on the grass, Curtis uncorked the bottle and poured four glasses of the sweet juice into each one. Slipping a little botulinum into three of the glasses, he gave them a swirl and walked over to the ladies, handing out the two glasses before going back to get the last two. They cheered to new friends and each raised their glass to their lips and swallowed the tainted wine.

He sat back as they chatted about current events until, one by one, the ladies fell asleep. That was too easy. He grabbed the scarves from his trunk and quickly wrapped them around their necks, pulling them tight. He waited until their breathing stopped and they lay motionless. He put them all in his car to take them to the desert to dispose of. He hoped when the local authorities found the car, they would mention the unopened wine bottle and the cheese that was left there. Surely that would not go unnoticed by his secret admirer.

After he disposed of the bodies in the Mojave Desert on his way back to Barstow, Curtis pulled into the yard to retrieve his rig and start his journey back east. He felt almost giddy and couldn't wait until the missing ladies would hit the news.

The news of the three ladies that disappeared without a trace after spending the day in Kingsland made national news. Every major network picked up the story. On the internet, the reference to the cheese left in the car did not go unnoticed and became the inspiration of numerous jokes about the ladies sharing wine and cheese. The cat-and-mouse game had officially begun.

Curtis sat back going about his daily activities, but secretly he got butterflies in his stomach every time he headed to the mailbox. Would a letter come today? Did they realize his response? On his nightly calls to Kaylee, she brought up the missing women. "The royal outing to Kingsland didn't end in the typical fairytale for them. There is lots of speculation as the local police are baffled. Whoever did this has obviously done it before. This was not an amateur."

He beamed with pride but was unable to take credit. He was content to silently bask in the knowledge that he was the greatest killer ever. One day, the world would know his name, but for now he kept it to himself, with the exception of his "playmate."

After several days, the leads dried up, and it was no longer headline news. Were his clues recognized? His answer came the very next day. In his mailbox lay an envelope from I.C. You. This time the postmark was from Los Angeles, California, home of Kingsland. He couldn't wait to open the envelope and discover what lay inside.

Tearing open the envelope and pulling out the letter, he felt like a little boy at Christmas. He hadn't felt this excited in a long time.

Curtis,

Well played, my friend, no lead to be found.

Bones are scattered over the sandy ground

Champaign cheddar left for all to see.

Crisp nectar in a bottle yet to be.

You showed you have skill and talent galore.

Is it time to even the score?

Be on the lookout for the trifecta finish

Where the ladies are dressed like the crowned British.

As the Beauty awaits, her Beast will appear,

And as always, know that I am near.

Curtis was mesmerized by the author. Were they telling him to kill again or was it their turn? Were they the Beast? Was he the Beast? This game certainly intrigued him. As he was contemplating his next move, the nightly news came on. The headline story caught his attention. "Three women were brutally murdered and their bodies left outside the racetrack, more details at five."

Horse racing was considered the sport of kings. The ladies certainly did dress like royalty at many events with the spectacular hats they wore. This must be what the note was referring to. But this killer was so brazen. They left the bodies to be found. Would they get caught? Would there be more, was this killer going to target him? So many questions and very few answers.

~ CHAPTER 11 ~

INTO THE FOLD

A few days later, another letter came in the mail. Hesitantly, he opened it, unprepared for what it said.

This game has started, to win the goal.

We both are brazen, we both are bold.

One lurks in the shadows, one out in the sun.

Both taste the blood just for fun.

Let's raise the ante and test the limits.

An eye for an eye, the secret no more.

It is now time to even the score

You hunt in a mask, you live in a myth.

I hunt with a sword that acts as my pen.

We both leave messages, each in our own way.

Combine we will, in a close day.

Tick tock the moon is waxing, the time draws near.

The blue light of knowledge will soon be clear.

Look close and look far, suspicion is near.

The land of red rock is where you met.

The natives are restless, and the game is set.

Eyes are on you, safety is gone.

The sword will find you, by the light of dawn.

Curtis knew instantly the tone had escalated. The urgency had shifted. He needed to act. He was now the hunted. He could only think of one person to confide in: Pappy. Hopping into his Mustang, he would call on the way.

When Curtis pulled into the drive of the old farmhouse, the stars were high in the sky and the moon was almost full. At least it was only the full moon in July, so there was still time. The porch light was on, and Tucker was inside, though he still barked at Curtis's arrival.

As Curtis walked up to the door with his bag in his hand, Pappy pushed open the front screen door. Grandma was sitting on the couch, and a plate of fresh baked cookies sat on the coffee table. "Grandma made you some cookies, and there is a plate warming in the oven for you, as I'm sure you didn't eat yet." Pappy knew him well.

Because he was focused on the letters and a brazen killer that had him in their crosshairs, food was the least of his concerns right now. "I am hungry, now that you mention it. I don't think I've eaten since breakfast." He headed to the kitchen, grabbing a couple cookies along the way.

Grandma smiled in approval. "You look exhausted. A good home-cooked meal hopefully will help while you talk with Pappy to work through your troubles."

Curtis knew that Pappy would never divulge his true secret and the source of his concern, but obviously he had prepared Grandma to understand that Curtis was troubled by something that he needed help working through. As he finished the plate of food, he said to Grandma, "That hit the spot. I really miss your cooking. One day you will have to teach Kaylee some of your recipes."

"I would like that very much," Grandma replied. "We need to have her over soon. She is such a nice girl, and you both seem very smitten and happy together. I like that."

Curtis smiled. "We will do that then. Real soon."

Pappy and Curtis headed out the back door to the shed. Once there, Curtis explained more of what had happened and pulled the folded letters from his pocket and laid them out on the workbench as they both pulled up stools and settled in. There was a lot to be analyzed.

Over the next few hours, they talked, analyzed, and speculated until they finally narrowed it down to a single plan. Pappy had never had anyone stalk him or even suggest that they knew his secret. Neither had Curtis. This was uncharted territory, one that needed to be carefully navigated. One false step and their whole world could come crashing down. They had devised a careful plan to catch a killer. They were ready to set their trap and wait for it to be sprung.

Curtis and Pappy had a well-thought-out plan to catch Curtis's nemesis. Tracking a nameless, faceless killer that they had no way of directly communicating with created a unique challenge, but they had one secret weapon: a witty journalist with an eye for the obscure that dabbled in darkness.

"Kaylee?" Curtis said into the phone. "I need you to come to Tennessee tomorrow. I know it's last minute, but I need your help."

"What is it? You are scaring me. Is everyone okay? Is it Pappy or Martha?" Kaylee inquired with a tremble in her voice.

"No, everyone is okay. I need your help. Something has come up, and Pappy and I need you here with us." Curtis responded in a calculated tone.

He knew that his cryptic rationale would both intrigued and terrify her. She loved this man and he trusted her. She answered with the only response that fit. "Did you already book my flight?"

"Of course I did, my love. First class. The seven o'clock out of O'Hare. I'll pick you up in Knoxville."

"I'll be there."

"Oh, and Kaylee?"

"Yes?"

"Thank you for trusting me."

"Absolutely, my love. See you soon." Kaylee hung up the phone.

As the sun started to set, Curtis headed to the airport to pick up the love of his life, and his soon-to-be partner in crime. As he pulled up, Kaylee stood at the curb with her small roller bag in tow. Her beautiful dark hair shone in the quickly fading light of the day. She eagerly waved as soon as she recognized his red Mustang. He slowed to a stop and hopped out. He grabbed her bag and gave her a quick peck as he hoisted her suitcase into the trunk before he jumped back in and they headed off.

"I must say, I was a little surprised at the urgency in your call. Not to mention the secrecy," Kaylee said.

"I will explain everything once we get to the house. There is a lot going on, but we are very grateful for your willingness to help."

"Of course. You know I have your back as I know you have mine."

As they pulled up to the old house, no one came out this time. They could see the light was on in the back shed, and they both knew it was from Pappy.

"I'll grab your bag and put it in my room. Grandma is out at bingo with her lady friends until later tonight, so no one will interrupt us. If you want to head to the shed, I know Pappy would be happy to see you."

Kaylee headed through the house towards the shed as Curtis put her things in the room he was staying in and grabbed a few bottles of soda. No alcohol tonight; they needed to keep their wits about them. This wasn't going to be an easy conversation. His hands shook as he carried the drinks. They both thought it would be better if Pappy started the conversation with Kaylee as Curtis was too close.

"Hi, Pappy!" Kaylee approached the open shed door. "Curtis told me to head out here while he was bringing my stuff in."

"Oh, Kaylee! So good to see you. Beautiful as ever, I might add." Pappy leaned over and gave her a small peck on the cheek.

Kaylee loved the Southern qualities of Curtis and his family. They were always so gracious and welcoming. She longed for that in her life and was grateful they provided it.

Pappy offered her a glass of sweet tea. "I'm sure you are wondering why we asked you here."

There was no need to wait for an answer, the nodding of her head was enough confirmation.

"Well, it seems as if our boy Curtis has found a secret admirer, and not the good kind. He has received some threatening letters, and this has us both more than a little concerned. I know that you have done some investigative reporting and broke some pretty hard cases wide open.

I've done a little digging myself, and I think we could really use your skills in this regard."

"Wow, Pappy, I didn't pit you as a fan of mine, but I'm flattered that you think so highly of my skills."

"Before we get too involved in the details, there is one thing that I need to let you in on. You see, the Mason family has always believed in justice. Sometimes things can be settled in a court of law, and sometimes they are better settled elsewhere, you understand?"

Kaylee nodded for him to go on.

"Crime, punishment, and love are three of the hardest words to understand. Crime happens in an instant, punishment needs to be swift, but love—love sustains, endures, overcomes. I know Curtis told you about his mother, Debra, and how we lost her. He told you about his dad and Candice and their roles."

Candice? Kaylee's antennae went up. Could it be? Could the unnamed mistress truly be Candice Jordon? Kaylee had suspected, but were they going to lay all the cards on the table? Right here in the shed where they brewed moonshine and hatched wild plans? Kaylee noted Pappy studying her. Had he dropped Candice's name on purpose? Was he testing her?

Kaylee was a skillful reporter and had perfected her poker face. The creases around Pappy's eyes deepened as a slight smile crept on his face. "When my daughter died at her own hand, there was no justice in the court system. Suicides aren't tried in a court of law, they are tried in the hearts of those left behind in the weeks, months, and years that follow as we try to pick up the pieces of shattered dreams and learn to live without them. When the actions of others were the triggers that caused the chain reaction that ultimately led to Debra's death, it was something that Curtis and I never could forgive. We couldn't accept it as 'God's will.' We wouldn't accept it. Curtis and I did what we needed to do to bring things right. To align the Universe again." Pappy paused.

"An eye for an eye," was all Kaylee said.

Kaylee hadn't noticed that Curtis had come to the shed and was standing by the door listening, watching her reaction, noting when she leaned in and sat up a little straighter when Pappy spoke Candice's name. He even thought he detected a little pride in her movements as the pieces fell into place. She knew his secret, and he was okay with that. At least she knew of this instance, perhaps not all the victims, but at least the first one. And the first one was always the hardest.

Feeling a little relieved, Curtis shuffled his feet, and Kaylee turned towards the door. When their eyes met, Curtis held his breath, searching her face for signs of acceptance, for a glimmer of hope that she was still by his side, that they would be okay. As their eyes locked, Kaylee's face remained motionless, expressionless. The air was heavy with silence. Their gazes fixed on each other; the rest of the world fell away as he searched for answers to questions they never wanted to ask. They saw each other for the first time, naked, unmasked. *How could you love a killer* was the thought that ran through his mind, and he suspected Kaylee's as well. Then he heard her voice inside his head answer him, *I can, and so can you.*

Puzzled, he stared into her eyes as he search for answers. Kaylee answered with her voice, "I, too, have delivered justice at my own hands. My stepfather was an evil man. May God have mercy on his soul."

Curtis looked at Pappy and saw him nod.

Kaylee broke the tension. "Are you just going to stand there? Pappy and I have a big mess to clean up thanks to you!" The jovial way in which she said it caused all of them to break out in laughter.

Pappy added in, "Looks like you definitely found a keeper in this pretty lady! And she's spot on with the mess you have created as well."

Curtis wrapped his arm around Kaylee's shoulders and pulled her in tight. "I couldn't agree more, Pappy!"

She reached up to kiss him.

"So how are we going to flush out this serpent that is causing us so much heartache?" Pappy said as they all gathered around the table.

~ CHAPTER 12 ~

UNEXPECTED EVENTS

Curtis and Kaylee woke up as the sunlight streamed through the bedroom windows of the plantation house. They had planned to spend the day working around the farm, tending to the gardens, checking on the calves, and doing some small maintenance items around the house. Curtis always liked to do most of the general maintenance himself and only hire out the big jobs.

As they were sitting at the breakfast bar finishing up their morning coffee, the phone rang. "Gosh, wonder who is calling so early?" Curtis picked up the phone. "Good morning, Pappy. Kaylee and I were just finishing up our coffee."

Kaylee yelled so he could hear her over the phone. "Good morning, Pappy."

Pappy replied with a sullen tone, "Good morning to both of you."

Suddenly, Curtis's brow furrowed as he noted the change in Pappy's tone.

Something was wrong. Kaylee stood and placed her hand on Curtis's shoulder as he listened.

"I'm sorry to call so early on a Saturday, but I needed to tell you that Grandma has taken a turn, and she is in the hospital. It doesn't look good, Curtis. I think you both need to come."

Without hesitation, Curtis responded, "Absolutely, we will leave now. Of course, we will be there soon. What hospital?"

"Mercy General," Pappy responded. "And Curtis? Please hurry."

"We will, Pappy. Tell Grandma we are on our way."

He hung up the phone and looked at Kaylee. She didn't need him to explain, she already knew. "You fix a cooler, and I'll pack a bag," Kaylee said.

Curtis just nodded. He was running on autopilot and going through the motions. Obediently, he went to the garage. As Kaylee headed upstairs to pack for them both, Curtis said out loud, "We just came back last night. How could this happen in just a few hours? We weren't supposed to go back for another few weeks."

Within thirty minutes, the Mustang was roaring down the highway towards Tennessee.

In record time, they pulled into the hospital parking lot and quickly found their way to Grandma's room. Entering the room and seeing the look of despair on Pappy's face was one of the hardest things that Curtis had endured.

Pappy hugged them both. "Grandma just fell asleep. She was trying to stay up to see you when you arrived, but she is just so weak."

"I'm glad she is getting some rest. She needs that to keep up her strength," Curtis responded as they sat down on the chairs in the room.

Kaylee looked around at the machines, lines, IV bag. So many numbers flashing on the monitor: heart rate, pulse, blood pressure, oxygen level. The constant beep of her heartbeat gave some solace that she was still with them. She looked so peaceful as she slept.

Pappy looked like he hadn't slept in days. "Pappy, when was the last time you ate?" Kaylee inquired.

"Umm, I had something for dinner last night, and I had a couple of bites of a danish this morning. I'm fine, not really very hungry."

"Pappy, you need to eat. I'll run down to the cafeteria and grab a couple of sandwiches for you both and some drinks. Be back in a second." Kaylee headed out the door.

Curtis had learned from Pappy that there was no use protesting once a woman made up her mind. That was it; it was nonnegotiable. They just nodded in unison.

"What do the doctors say?" Curtis asked Pappy.

"It's not good. They said that all her organs are failing. She is not coming home. They said days, maybe a week, at most. I've watched so many people die in my life, but this is the hardest. I'm not prepared to say goodbye to her. Martha is my lifeblood. She is the reason I get up in the morning. She is the first person I see in the morning and the last one before I close my eyes. How will I go on without her? What is my purpose? How will I learn to live without her? I'm not sure I want to." Pappy closed his eyes, his head fell into his hands, and he wept.

Curtis wasn't sure how to respond. He probably didn't need to respond. He just hugged Pappy. There were no words. There was no need. Pappy's words hung thick in the air. The love between them inspired so many over the years. Curtis longed for that kind of connection with someone. He thought he could have that with Kaylee, but he wasn't sure.

Pappy had figured out that he was worthy of deep, meaningful love. Martha was able to love a killer, albeit she didn't know, at least according to Pappy. Curtis wasn't so sure.

"I only wish to one day have what you and Grandma have. That is true unconditional love. You are soulmates. Even if she is no longer in this world, she will always be by your side until you are together again."

Pappy looked up at Curtis. "You are a very wise young man. You may not realize now, but you need to hold onto that girl of yours. She is special in ways that you may not yet know. I have seen it in the stars. You will always be connected."

He knew not to question Pappy's visions. They were never wrong. A smile came upon his lips as he thought of spending his life with Kaylee. That made him happy.

They sat silently with the beep of Grandma's heart monitor keeping rhythm with her breaths. Two beeps, breathe in, one beep hold, two beeps out. The methodical pace gave them hope that she had stabilized.

Kaylee broke their trance as she returned with food. "I grabbed a couple of sandwiches, salad, drinks, and some cookies. Not nearly as good as Grandma's, but they looked yummy." She placed them on the tray over the end of the bed.

She unwrapped each sandwich, handing one gently to first Pappy then Curtis. Slowly, they raised their heads. "You both look pale as ghosts! I think I got back just in time."

Curtis and Pappy blinked the moisture from their bloodshot eyes, both quietly muttered a barely audible, "Thanks."

Kaylee helped herself to the last sandwich and took her rightful place beside Curtis.

His hands visibly shook as he slowly lifted the sandwich to his lips, forcing himself to take a bite.

Kaylee reached over and gently placed her hand on his leg. He managed a slight smile to acknowledge her gesture of support. She was special, in so many ways.

Nurses shuffled in and out. The three sat vigilantly as they shared stories, anecdotes, with each other, with Grandma. Stories of happier times, memorable moments, shared secrets. Evidence of a life well lived. As the hours went on and the room became dark, the conversation dwindled until the only sound was the beeping heart rate monitor and the sound of Grandma's breathing.

Curtis counted the beeps. The rhythm had slowed. Her song was coming to an end. Sometime in the night, Martha Mason left this world peacefully, surrounded by her family, holding her beloved's hand.

The sound of the solid, cold beep stirred Curtis from his slumber. Pappy held her hand and simply whispered, "Goodbye, my love, until we meet again." He kissed her hand and her cheeks as the heart rate monitor ended on a steady long beep.

The nurse quickly came in to turn it off and confirmed the passing.

~ CHAPTER 13 ~

The Plan

Curtis and Kaylee awoke in the huge plantation bed still tired from the recent events. The days spent at the hospital followed by the funeral took their toll. Slowly, they made their way downstairs to the kitchen as they hoped a couple strong cups of coffee would energize them.

Curtis grabbed the stack of mail neatly piled on the counter and started sorting it, suddenly stopping at one letter. The color drained from his face as his hands shook. The address was to Grandma's name care of Curtis MacIntyre.

His gasp caught Kaylee's attention. Quickly turning around, she saw the letter. "What the fuck?" was all she could muster.

"What does this mean? You don't think…" Curtis couldn't even finish the thought. The idea that this monster had anything to do with Grandma's passing was insurmountable.

"Open it." Kaylee's voice was a quiet whisper.

Curtis's hands trembled with fear and anticipation of what the words inside would reveal. Slowly, he tore open the envelope and revealed a card. Bewildered, he pulled out the card and read the front out loud. "With deepest sympathy on the loss of your grandmother." When he opened the card, a folded note fell out. He read the inside message. "Very few can understand the deep sadness you are experiencing now. May you find comfort in the memories you have." He picked up the folded letter and read it out loud.

As death creeps closer, time draws short.
The blue moon's approach marks the day in court.

Did she die of natural causes, did someone intervene?

The questions you have seldom are seen.

Sitting silently through the night.

All eyes shut tight.

The serpent approaches, and no one hears.

To end the life amid all the fears.

So close yet out of reach.

The one you cannot catch.

For in the darkness that night

I was hiding in plain sight.

Try as you might I can get to you.

You are too smart not to follow the clues.

We both have seen the face of death many times before.

Now is the time to even the score.

Tick tock the countdown draws near.

The energy spills from within the sphere.

The gun is loaded, the hammer cocked,

The crosshairs are scanning, the target is locked.

Who's in the scope is anyone's guess.

Checkmate is near in this game of chess.

Curtis's brow furrowed as his head dropped. His entire body trembled as he finally looked up at Kaylee. In unison they both said, "We need Pappy."

"Great minds think alike." He felt a bit of hope.

As they packed their bags, Curtis made a call to Pappy telling him they were on their way and the Serpent had sent them a note.

The moon was high in the sky when they pulled into the familiar drive. The porch light shone brightly, and they could hear Tucker's familiar bark from inside. Pappy met them at the door and ushered them to the kitchen table. "No need to head to the shed. Tucker will keep our secrets."

Curtis laid out the most recent letter he received along with the card that came with it. After what seemed like an eternity, Pappy spoke. "We will never truly know the answer if they had a hand in Martha's death. What I do know is there will be consequences for suggesting they did. Curtis, remember the conversations we had about 'an eye for an eye'? Well, this is that time. We need to lure them in and strike first. This will be our greatest battle. Someone will not come back from this fight. It needs to be them."

"Agreed. The reference to 'red rock where you met,' why is he luring us back?" Pappy rubbed his head.

"Curtis and I actually met in Winslow," Kaylee corrected him as she reached for the letter. "Something about these lines." She read them aloud. "*The land of red rock is where you met/The natives are restless, and the game is set/Eyes are on you, safety is gone/The sword will find you, by the light of dawn.* I get the reference to Arizona and the red rock of Sedona. The natives, does that refer to the Hopi tribe and the ruins we visited?"

"Could be. Keep talking it out, I think you're on to something." Curtis urged her to continue.

"What about the line from the card, '*Tick tock the countdown draws near/The energy spills from within the sphere*'? What is that referring to?" Pappy questioned as he leaned forward pointing to the card.

As she thought about the energy and sphere reference, Kaylee's eye grew brighter as she realized the connection.

Curtis noted it immediately. "What is running around in that brain of yours?"

"The Sedona area is known for its metaphysical movement. The energy swirls up from the earth or into the earth depending on where you are. It is sought out as a place for self-discovery and enlightenment. It is said to transform lives," Kaylee explained.

"Arizona it is. All roads lead back there. That is where we need to do battle. Where we will ultimately win," Curtis responded.

The trio sat silently in the car as the miles counted down until they reached Flagstaff, Arizona. Curtis gazed out the windshield across the desert abyss as the enormity of what lay ahead weighed heavy. He glanced over at Kaylee as she diligently worked on a freelance article. He knew her mind worked best when busy. This article was just the distraction she needed in the third and final day of their cross-country trek. He knew she was his soulmate, his future. The one who made him whole.

His thoughts drifted back to Kaylee's comments about Sedona, that it was a place of self-discovery. He found that eerily unnerving. Curtis had never killed with a partner and certainly not his grandfather or Kaylee. Kaylee had only killed once. The unease of this venture into the unknown was both exhilarating and concerning.

Curtis sang along with the radio as he tried to drown out the sound of his heartbeat pounding in his ear as the miles clicked off to their final destination. He glanced in the rearview mirror.

Stretched out comfortably in the back seat of the Mustang, Pappy looked off in the distance, mindlessly stroking his faithful dog, Tucker, who laid beside him, his chin perched on Pappy's thigh.

Curtis knew this pose well. Tucker gazed up at his master, ready to respond when asked. Dogs had a psychic ability to read people's minds. Even Pappy's private ways were no match for his trusted dog. Tucker always knew what his master thought or felt, often before he did. His diligent, watchful stance signaled he was ready to stand by Pappy in the fight that lay ahead.

Curtis glanced over to Kaylee and laughed. *There's my faithful dog.*

"What's so funny?" Kaylee set her article aside.

"I was just thinking about how we should all aspire to unconditional love," Curtis said as she patted her leg.

Curtis laughed even louder when Kaylee responded, "Woof, woof." They were meant to be together.

As they entered the city of Flagstaff, all three of them and the dog sat up straighter, eyes scanning the houses searching for the blue house numbered 236, signaling they had arrived. Turning into the drive, Pappy was the first to speak. "Let's get settled in and meet up in a bit. Let the games begin!"

Kaylee and Curtis jumped out, gathered the bags, and headed towards the door. Curtis would never allow Pappy to carry his own bag in. His mother taught him better than that. You must respect your elders. Gathered around the small, round table in the kitchen of the rented house, Curtis anxiously flipped the pen through his fingers while Kaylee picked at her nail polish.

As Pappy entered, they both looked straight at him. His mere presence commanded attention, a respect earned through years of leadership, perseverance, and conquered hardships. Life didn't always come easy for Pappy. His pride often got in the way, and the years of secrecy had taken a toll. The loss of Martha just a few weeks prior left a wound that was deep and still very raw. The thought that someone, anyone, had a hand in her sudden departure would not go without a response. Just as he and Curtis avenged Deb's death, they most certainly sought retribution for Martha's.

As they pieced together what they knew about the Serpent, Kaylee went over the profile she had compiled. "The Serpent is most likely a man, mid-thirties to early forties, highly educated and most likely has a public job. His preference to display his victims publicly in highly visible locations shows he seeks external recognition. He draws energy from outwitting those searching for him. He leaves clues that are very obscure and is confident that few, if any, will find them. This makes him feel even more superior, powerful, and confident. He is threatened by us as we detect his clues and leave our own. The fact that he found Curtis and was able to potentially get close enough to Martha shows he is able to blend in and appear very trustworthy. He will be close by, observing us, as he likes to hide in plain sight. He respects those that do and feels he is better than Curtis, as he sees him as someone who hides in the shadows."

"Do you think he knows about Pappy?" Curtis asked.

They looked at each other, silently contemplating the question.

Pappy spoke first. "I believe he knows that you have confided in me, but I don't think he knows of my past."

Kaylee nodded her head. "I agree. I think that Pappy can definitely be used to our advantage. He would believe that Pappy is weak and feeble and easy to overtake, which could not be further from the truth. Perhaps we need to exploit that and portray Pappy as being so distraught over the loss of Martha that he just couldn't be left alone and that is why he is here. Pappy can be the silent observer from the sideline without raising any suspicion."

"That's a good plan, Kaylee," Curtis responded. "Keep the focus on me and you, and Pappy is just along for the ride."

They spent the rest of the afternoon huddled around the table as they hashed out the fine details of their plan. As the trio headed out for their first public appearance, Pappy said, "All the world's a stage, and we are merely actors."

"And this will be our best performance ever!" Kaylee took Curtis's hand and kissed Pappy's cheek. They walked to a local restaurant in downtown Flagstaff, Kaylee and Curtis hand in hand with their fingers intertwined. They reminisced about how they first met on a trip to Flagstaff. Pappy, his head bowed, shoulders hunched ever so slightly, shuffled along a few steps back. As they approached the restaurant, Curtis pulled open the door, and Kaylee bounded through as she waited a moment for Pappy to catch up.

As they took their seats at the table, the conversation continued about Kaylee and Curtis's first meeting in Winslow.

Pappy quickly scanned the menu and then the room. They all looked for someone ordinary, nondescript, but definitely alert. Curtis knew he would show up. Maybe not tonight, maybe not in this restaurant, but he would make an appearance. When he does, they will be watching.

Kaylee broke the silence. "Oooo, I think I may have the salmon. It sounds really good."

Curtis responded. "Perfect. Then I can have the prime rib and we can share. Surf and turf. I knew there was a reason I brought you along." Curtis laughed, followed by his signature eyebrow nod that Kaylee had told him she found so endearing. "What looks good to you, Pappy?"

"I'm not too hungry, but I was leaning towards a steak as well. Maybe just the filet. I don't think I could eat the prime rib."

The waiter arrived and took their order, leaving bread and butter on the table.

Kaylee talked about heading down to Sedona tomorrow. "There was a nice downtown area where

Pappy could hang out and maybe we could hike or bike in the hills a bit before it gets too hot."

"That sounds like a good idea. We could check out the healing power of the vortex. You up for that, Pappy?" Curtis asked.

"Sure, sounds fine. I could use a little healing myself." Pappy's head was still lowered as he looked at the menu.

They all continued to scan the room, looking for their unknown guest. Kaylee spied him first.

A man walked casually into the restaurant and headed over to the bar area after speaking with the maître d'. He took a seat at a high-top table immediately next to the dining room, with a clear sight line to most of the tables. He was tall, probably close to six feet, medium build, wearing jeans and a dark-green shirt. His hair was cut short, and he had on a baseball hat pulled low over his eyes, which shielded most of his face from view.

Normally, he would not draw a second glance from her, but under the circumstances alarm bells rang loudly in her ears. She excused herself to the restroom, which was their code for a person of interest was noticed. "I think the restroom is just inside the bar." She asked one of the servers, and they confirmed its location and off she headed. As she walked by the mysterious man, he was reading the menu, his head lowered and the baseball hat still in place, obstructing her view of his face.

Curtis and Pappy turned, watching her navigate through the tables of diners and enter the bar, taking a quick note of the stranger.

While Kaylee was gone, Curtis asked, "Could it be?"

"I'm not sure," Pappy replied. "Fits the profile, that's for sure. Best keep a keen eye out and enjoy this amazing dinner with your beautiful lady."

When Kaylee rejoined them, she asked, "Did you miss me?"

"Always! My dear, always." Curtis leaned in to give her a quick peck on the cheek.

"Have you ever been to Sedona, Kaylee?" Pappy kept the conversation going.

"I have but haven't had a chance to do a lot of sightseeing in the mountains and canyons. It's such a beautiful and unique landscape."

"The red rocks of Sedona are legendary. Lots of stories in them hills. Not like in the Smokies, but still. Sacred places, too, for the Native Americans," Pappy added

As they finished up their dessert, the stranger in the bar finished his meal and made his way out of the restaurant. It didn't go unnoticed that as he glanced around the dining room, he hesitated just a second when he came to their table. Subtle but for the keen observer, discernible. Curtis noted the observation. "Well, our visitor definitely knows we are here."

"You saw that too?" Kaylee asked.

"Yes, ma'am." Curtis described it for Pappy, as his back was towards the door. "His glance paused just a fraction of a second at our table, before he turned away and exited."

"Interesting, son. Wonder if he found what he was looking for? At least I hope he enjoyed a good meal, as it may be one of his last."

The next morning, the trio got up early and drove down to Sedona as planned. Kaylee grabbed her big sun hat as they headed out. The car quickly filled with the smell of coconuts from the copious amount of suntan lotion they had applied. The scenery out the window quickly changed from high- to mid-desert vegetation as Humphreys Peak grew smaller in the rearview mirror and the red rocks of Sedona appeared on the horizon.

Curtis's thoughts drifted to the man at the restaurant last night as he guided the red Mustang through traffic. He recalled each detail, his clothes, his mannerisms, the slight upcurl of his lip as they made eye contact last night. He didn't say anything to the others about the sneer aimed at him as their eyes locked last night. The knot in his stomach reminded him that this was all too real.

Thankfully, he inherited his mother's intuition. The peaceful strength he felt when he sternly met his eyes, he knew instinctively his mom was there, protecting him, providing him guidance and strength to slay this demon.

His fingers repeatedly gripped and released the steering wheel, his jaw clenched, and his breathing deepened and slowed. His fingers constantly flicked and tapped as he struggled to make sense of all this.

Kaylee gently reached over and laid her hand on his thigh. Her touch instantly brought him back to the present.

Curtis looked over at her and smiled. She knew him too well. That's what he loved about her; she knew the real Curtis, and despite all his flaws, she accepted him unconditionally. Curtis dreamed of his soulmate, his partner in crime, someone who could see the monster behind the mask and not shy away. She was strong yet gentle, forceful and powerful when needed but was comfortable being his wingman. He knew he could count on her. No matter what they encountered, he knew he was a better man with her by his side.

He also knew she would not overtly ask him what he contemplated, but she subtly cued him that she was aware of his internal struggle. He needed to share it with her but wasn't sure it was the right time. When would be the right time? Would there ever be a right time? What would Debra say to him? As a smile came across his face, he knew the answer even before he asked himself the question.

"No time like the present." Curtis broke the silence in the car. Looking in the rearview mirror, he could see Pappy's face, his brow furrowed, his lips pursed, his eyes longing to understand what he would say next. Curtis glanced at Kaylee, a smile on her face, eyes wide and her lips slightly parted, as if inviting him to speak. Her hand lightly patted his thigh.

"Last night at the restaurant, the mystery bar man definitely was there for us." He paused a moment. "When he was leaving, he looked straight at me. I don't know if you noticed, but we locked eyes for a second. I felt like he was trying to peer into my soul. To understand my innermost thoughts, fears, dreams. As if to say, I see you. Just like his letters. A cold shiver went through my body, and then he curled the corner of his mouth ever so slightly, as a final slap in the face. It was definitely him."

Pappy and Kaylee sat motionless in the car.

Pappy was the first to speak. "I thought it was. You seemed a bit shaken as we headed back to the house. He is very brazen and daring. Definitely—what did he say?—likes to hide in plain sight. I'd say ball's in our court now. We all need to stay alert at all times, as I'm sure he'll be close by, ready to strike. Most likely without warning."

"Do you think it's a good idea to split up today?" Kaylee asked.

"I think we stick to the plan, but I'll stay in a public area. Maybe hang at a restaurant. An outdoor cafe would make a good choice."

"Yes. I think we still go on a ride, but maybe keep it to an hour at most. We will keep our walkie-talkies out so we are in constant communication," Curtis said.

"Good thinking, babe." Kaylee smiled at Curtis.

"Let the games begin! Ooohhh, this is going to get fun. I can't wait!" Pappy rubbed his hands together like a young boy getting ready for his birthday party.

—————————●—————————

Once in Sedona, Kaylee and Curtis walked off to rent a couple mountain bikes while Pappy headed to a local cafe with tables outside. He found a table, thankful that the restaurant was busy. He situated his chair so he could see the entire street with the building wall at his back. He ordered a coffee and a pastry, and he meticulously scanned the crowds as they walked up and down the street. He wouldn't possibly be so bold as to wear that baseball hat again, or would he?

The air was filled with children's laughter, interspersed with an occasional attempt of a parent trying fruitlessly to rein in their excitement of the pending day's activities. The morning breeze brushed against Pappy's cheek as it brought the smell of freshly brewed coffee and baked goods that would soon grace his table.

Bright colors flashed by in his peripheral vision as visitors and locals went about their daily tasks. The sidewalks were filled with singles, couples, families, even the occasional dog. Sunglasses and hats were the staple for all, and those that were lacking this attire stood out more than those that had donned them.

Pappy scanned the crowds looking for the little too ordinary. Someone who blended and stood out at the same time. He was a master at this cat-and-mouse game. This was his favorite part.

Although he approached his seventy-seventh year of life, he still had a lot on his bucket list. He wanted to see Curtis marry. He wanted to meet his first great-grandchild. He wanted peace for his wife and himself. He hoped to experience all of these things. Time, precious time, now more than ever. He heard the ever-present tick of the clock in his head. The life clock that everyone had and few listened to. It had kept pace with him for a long time. The tick had gotten louder lately, made its presence known. Most would think that a life clock might grow fainter with time, but with each revolution it grew ever closer to the fatal time when it would stop. For those that listened with the intent to understand, attuned to the subtle changes in the Universe, and focused on internal and external loci of control, the signals were deafening at times, shouting, unmistakable, and an ever-present reminder of our own immortality.

As Pappy brought the steaming cup to his lips, air exited his lips ever so slightly in a vain attempt to cool the hot liquid housed inside. His nostrils inhaled deeply the calming aroma of the caffeinated beverage.

His eyes peered up, squinting, trying to keep the steam at bay, as a man entering his field of vision caught his attention. Tall, black sunglasses, short hair, dressed in black shorts, a blue T-shirt, and red sneakers. What was it about this guy that drew his glance? His head was pointed straight ahead, a smile on his face as he maneuvered through the crowds. No one with him, and he walked with purpose. A man on a mission.

He continued down the street until he entered a pharmacy on the corner. Maybe he was on an errand, maybe he was not their Serpent. But what if he was? Pappy did not take a chance. He continued to watch, ever aware of those coming and going from the pharmacy. Could there be a separate entrance? It was on the corner after all. Perhaps there was a way for him to exit out the back.

He grabbed his walkie-talkie as he headed towards the corner. A smile shot across his face all the way up to his eyes as he turned the corner and walked down to the edge of the building. The back door led not to an alley but to a city park. A nice grassy area directly behind the line of businesses that edged the street. What a nice day for a walk in the park, Pappy said to himself as he finished off the last sip of coffee.

Quickly keying the mic, he simply said, "Heading to the park. Glad I didn't bring my red sneakers with all this walking." As he rounded the corner of the pharmacy, Kaylee and Curtis approached from the other direction. They would arrive first. This ambush could end one of two ways: very good or very, very bad.

Curtis and Kaylee slowed as they approached the park, chatting about her latest article to avoid suspicion.

Pappy scanned the groups gathered in the park: families with little kids over by the swings, a man with his dog near the trees.

On the bench reading a sports magazine was the man with the red shoes. Nonchalantly, he flipped through the pages at a pace that denoted he was clearly not reading the text. Back and forth, the pages flipped, over and over much like a restless child or a relative waiting in a hospital for an update on their loved one.

As Curtis and Kaylee rode by, the stranger's eyes didn't appear to notice them. He wouldn't let on with all of them approaching. Pappy entered the park from the far end just as they passed the park bench, noting the man turn his head quickly, watching where they went.

Kaylee and Curtis continued down the path to the other end of the park and stopped at a water fountain and began refilling their water bottles on the bikes.

While the man's head was turned, Pappy grabbed a seat on a nearby bench in the shade and watched, waited. "Check. It's your move."

The chess game that ensued involved the three of them surrounding the Serpent, only to watch him walk away, giving a nod to them as he walked passed. Taunting them, so close yet out of reach. After hours of this, Pappy and Curtis were growing frustrated. They decided to get some lunch and then take their leave, knowing that their opponent would follow.

As they headed back to Flagstaff, the trio actively discussed the day's events. "We know who he is now. He even lowered his sunglasses several times as we passed. Tomorrow is a new day, and this will be checkmate. I can feel it," Curtis declared.

Curtis felt the adrenaline rush from his words. They all wanted the same thing, to slay the Serpent, but all for different reasons. Pappy looked to avenge Grandma's death. He needed to win against the best. And Kaylee, she wanted to feed her dark side, he was certain.

Would the Serpent be able to satisfy all of their separate desires? Could one person or one kill provide for all of them? Like lionesses on the hunt, they worked together for a common cause and for the survival of the pack. The kill itself represented nourishment, fuel to keep them going. It replenished their lifeblood; it fed their souls. This would be the first time they worked as a team. It may very well be the last. The beginning of the end or a start of a new beginning; sometimes they were indistinguishable.

With the sun's rays peeking over the horizon and the sky ablaze with colors of a new day, Curtis and Pappy enjoyed their morning coffee on the deck while Kaylee put the final touches on their breakfast feast. As she opened the door from the kitchen, they were greeted with the smell of bacon. "Bacon, eggs, with some sausage on the side. The toast will be right up," she said cheerfully as she turned back to grab the rest of the food.

"Mmm mm. You certainly outdid yourself this morning, little lady." Pappy eyed the bacon while he reached for the sausage. "I don't think I've enjoyed a breakfast this good since Martha passed."

The statement still stung. It had been a month but seemed like only yesterday. Curtis knew the power of revenge to ease that sorrow. He yearned for Pappy to feel that as well. He planned to let Pappy have the final blow, so to speak, if he could. Pappy deserved it.

~ CHAPTER 14 ~

TRUE LOVE KILLS TOGETHER

After breakfast, the three headed out to a local forest north of the city. It was high in elevation and served mainly primitive campers, so the foot traffic was minimal. They were certain their mystery man would show up. He was hellbent to see this game through. As the Mustang's engine roared to life, the sun crept ever higher in the sky.

Kaylee closed her eyes, bowed her head, and said a little prayer silently.

As they pulled into the parking lot, there were only a few cars there, and from the remnants of morning dew and leaves on them, they had been parked overnight.

They got out of the car and proceeded to understand the lay of the land. Curtis and Pappy checked their packs to make sure their gear was readily available. No trace left behind. As they headed off down one of the trails on foot carrying their backpacks, the sounds of birds chirping filled the air.

"I love the sounds of nature. It's so relaxing and welcoming," Kaylee said.

"You can tell so much by the animals and their patterns," Curtis added.

"Yes, I remember from our conversations when we first met. Funny, we've come full circle. Again, reading the signs from nature." Kaylee grabbed his hand and swung it joyfully as they walked down the path. The crushed granite dust crackled under their feet as they continued their trek into the forest. The path wound around the parking lot before it turned and headed off into the trees. They knew there were two other lots they would pass along their journey. As they passed the first one, they paused to look for new cars, but none were there.

As their hopes were challenged, Kaylee questioned, "Are you sure he will show?"

"He will be here all right. He is all in like a pig at breakfast, my love," he responded with his fake Southern accent.

"A pig at breakfast? What are you talking about?" Kaylee questioned in her annoyed voice he knew all too well.

"You have never heard that? Well, a chicken contributes to the meal, she gives an egg, but the pig, the pig is fully committed as evidenced by the delicious bacon you fried up for us this morning. He is definitely a pig and not a chicken."

"Yep. He's a pig alright! A pig about to get slaughtered." Pappy laughed.

As they approached the second lot, there was a small white car in the lot that appeared to have just arrived. The cooling metal of its hood sent tapping sounds into the air. They walked over to take a closer look.

Pappy held his hand over the hood. "Yep. It's definitely a new arrival. Let's hope it belongs to Mr. Red Shoes."

Kaylee glanced into the car. Neat, orderly, an empty plastic bottle in the drink holder and interestingly, a pair of red sneakers thrown on the passenger's seat.

"He must have changed his shoes. There are the red sneakers." Kaylee pointed through the passenger's window. They all peered in.

"Interesting," was all Pappy said.

As they looked over at the trail leading into the woods, Curtis took a deep breath and exhaled loudly. "Let's do this." He led them into battle.

They all took a deep breath and headed off after their leader.

Kaylee noticed Curtis almost skipping and prancing along as they entered the trees. The song "Heigh-Ho" with the vision of the seven dwarfs entered her head and caused her to laugh. "You seem entirely too chipper."

"And that surprises you? This is what I do, this is who I am."

In that moment, the reality of the events struck her head-on. They were headed to kill a monster. How could you kill a monster without becoming one yourself? The thought terrified her. This was no different than her stepfather. It was kill or be killed. She tried to convince herself as they walked.

Uneasiness sat in the pit of her stomach. It was a sign of difficult times to come. She wasn't sure what, but she could sense the time was close.

Curtis brushed his palms against his shorts, wiping the moisture away. Kaylee watched, observing his every move for clues. He would pause, turn his head to the side slightly, signaling he heard something. Kaylee would stop and listen for sounds of sticks cracking or leaves rustling. She could sense he was close. She knew Curtis could feel it too. The Serpent's eyes watched them, but from where? Curtis clearly searched the woods with every sense he had but returned nothing.

Pappy and Kaylee lagged behind, knowing their place. This was Curtis's fight. They were merely support, the second string. The Serpent had called him to arms, taunted him relentlessly, poked and prodded, until finally it had come to this. He loved puzzles and mind games. This was the ultimate prize. To claim victory against a fellow monster, a demon, a killer, this would be Curtis's ultimate prize. For Kaylee, the thought of what lay ahead was exhilarating, frightening, and even a little erotic.

As they approached a clearing in the woods, they saw an outcropping of rocks to the left.

"Must be over there." Pappy pointed towards the jagged rocks.

Off the path towards the rocky edge, there were large boulders embedded in the dirt. Moss grew on some and made the footing slippery. "Careful, Pappy. It's getting a little treacherous." Kaylee paused so he could catch up. She extended her hand.

He grabbed it, steadying himself as he navigated the rocky terrain. Pappy got around well for a man of his age, but at times, the toll it had taken on his body was very visible. Pappy kept ahold of Kaylee's hand.

"Kaylee." He was almost whispering. "I'm glad Curtis found you. He is very lucky, we both are. You are good for each other. I see a future for you two." He raised her hand to his lips and kissed it ever so gently. "And for that I am glad. We are very blessed."

"Thank you, Pappy. That means the world to me. I feel lucky to have you both in my life, hopefully for a very long time."

Curtis suddenly stopped and held up his hand, his palm faced them, fingers outstretched. He trembled yet stood tall. The birds had stopped chirping. The world was silent; time stood still.

Kaylee held her breath, her eyes fixed on Curtis as his eyes darted, scanning the area.

"The Serpent was here. He was right here, ready to strike," Curtis said quietly

Pappy and Kaylee's eyes were fixed on Curtis. Kaylee had never seen him like this. A fierce warrior, tall, strong, confident, the blood pulsed through his veins, visible in his neck and his biceps. Her mouth fell open in awe of such a magnificent creature. He was man, hear him roar was never truer than in this very moment. Everything she ever hoped, everything she wanted, and even what she didn't know she wanted stood before her. At this precise second, the Universe showed her what she already knew: She was meant to be with Curtis, she was meant to share his life, good, bad. She had seen the man behind the mask and she was not afraid. He was hers.

Glancing at Pappy, Kaylee could see the pride sparkling in his eyes as he watched his grandson, his lifeblood, his daughter's son, poised, ready. Pride that only a father, grandfather could feel when the student surpassed the teacher.

Both Kaylee's and Pappy's eyes were fixed on Curtis. They watched helplessly as his lips parted in slow motion, words beginning to form as his face distorted, taking on a demonic quality. His muscles rippled under his shirt as he expertly swung around and lunged past them both. Simultaneously, they both ducked, and Kaylee ran forward, dropping Pappy's hand.

Pappy raised his arm over his head like a shield as he spun around. The Serpent connected the pipe with Pappy's arm and head. Blood dripped down his face towards his mouth.

"NNNNOOOOOO!!!!!" Curtis bellowed, lunging towards him, connecting just after the mighty blow.

Kaylee's screams rang out.

Blood splattered from the gash on Pappy's head, and bones cracking echoed through the trees as the iron pipe connected with his flesh. He stumbled to regain his balance; rage burned bright in Pappy's eyes. He might be old, but he was not feeble. Blinking, Pappy touched the wound on his skull and looked at the resulting blood on his right hand. His left forearm hung awkwardly at his side.

Curtis knocked the Serpent back and had him pinned against a tree, his hands fiercely gripping his neck. Kaylee watched, mesmerized, frozen unable to move. The Serpent swung the pipe at Curtis, blows that repeatedly landed on his head and back.

Curtis stared into the killer's eyes, never blinking. His hands wrapped around his throat. The muscles flexed on Curtis's forearms; the more his prey struggled, the tighter he squeezed. The veins in his arms bulged as they pumped more and more blood towards his hands. His fingers dug into the man's throat. His arms shook as he applied upward pressure, bringing the victim's weight off his feet ever so slightly.

As he gasped for breath, the Serpent's limbs swung wildly, fighting for his life. Kaylee could not look away. He would not give up easily.

Curtis's face grew more and more furious. His features were distorted. "You will die! Fucking bastard, I will be the last one you see!"

Pappy stopped and watched his prodigy squeeze the life out of this man.

Kaylee, on her knees, watched in awe as the man she loved took another life in front of her. She felt the need to pray, although not a religious person. She begged God to have mercy on their souls. She prayed for Curtis, for Pappy, for herself, and even for the Serpent.

Curtis never faltered. He stared into the Serpent's eyes, never diverting, waiting patiently until the light of life was extinguished. Snuffed out by his hands.

The Serpent stood motionless for several minutes, being held up solely by Curtis's grasp. Trancelike, Curtis lowered his head. Tilting his head to the side, his face took on a childlike appearance as he gazed in bewilderment at the dead man that hung at the end of his arms. His lips pursed, and his brow furrowed. He squared his shoulders and stood tall.

Pappy came forward and placed his hand on Curtis's shoulder. "You've done good, my boy," he said quietly. "You made me proud." He patted his grandson's shoulder.

Kaylee wasn't so sure what she felt. She was glad they were safe. She was terrified at what lay ahead. What were they doing with this body? How could they get away with it? She knew this was not their first rodeo, and they knew what to do. But could she keep the secret? Could she sleep at night knowing she watched the man she loved kill someone? Could she ever forget the devil, the demon she saw?

"It was in self-defense, Kaylee," Pappy stated as if he read her mind. "I have the wounds to prove it."

"Are we calling the police?"

Curtis and Pappy looked at each other and then laughed. "Call the police? I don't think I've ever thought of that as an option before."

"Hey, there's a first time for everything, Curtis. Maybe we should?"

They sat in the woods as Kaylee went to the payphone in the parking lot and dialed 911. The police and EMTs arrived quickly. The sound of news choppers circled overhead as well. Kaylee made sure this would be on the evening news. Curtis would be a headline. She wrote her Pulitzer Prize–winning story in her head as they waited. The EMTs transported Pappy to the nearest hospital, and Kaylee and Curtis quickly followed.

The police detective was waiting for them when they arrived and questioned them both while Pappy was being examined. The doctor came out to talk to them and said he was very concerned. Pappy was much more critical than he appeared. The pressure was building up in his brain, and they needed to relieve it quickly or risk permanent damage, even death.

Kaylee and Curtis were stunned.

"How can that be? He is talking and walking." Kaylee shook her head trying to make sense of what the doctor was telling them.

"Brain injuries are tricky. They can be very serious without a lot of outward signs. He is heading to imaging, and then he will go to surgery. The orthopedic will also set his arm while he is under so we don't risk another surgery. He is in a very fragile state."

They both nodded and reached for each other, wrapped their arms tightly around each other in an effort to support and protect. Kaylee buried her face in Curtis's chest as she started to sob. Curtis stood tall, slowly nodded at the doctor as he rubbed Kaylee's back. Inhaling, he responded, "Thank you, doctor. Take care of Pappy. He is all we have."

"I will do my best." He turned away and swiftly disappeared down the hall through the swinging doors.

~ CHAPTER 15 ~

The Eulogy

Kaylee stared out the big picture window that overlooked the back gardens at MacIntyre Plantation. After Pappy's death, Curtis asked her to stay in North Carolina indefinitely. Her computer screen shone brightly in front of her, the pages of words, thoughts, and stories that made up Darryl Mason's life filled the screen.

"How could a life so well lived be summarized in less than twenty-five hundred words?" Kaylee asked as she penned a feature article about Pappy, how he lived and how he died.

"That day in the forest, no one thought for a moment that the Serpent would have dealt the final blow that ultimately ended this great man's life. The only comfort was that his killer's life also ended that day," Curtis began. "That day in the woods. I looked in his eyes. I saw my reflection in his pupils."

Kaylee looked away from her computer and focused on Curtis. "What did you see?" Her voice shook as she recalled the vivid memory of the demonic persona she saw that day.

"What I saw scared me. I had never seen my face when I killed before. I focused on the others, their expressions."

Kaylee reached over and touched his hand. "I saw it too. The monster within. How can one kill a monster without becoming one themselves?"

"I know what Mom meant by 'the demons were near.' I have seen the demon, face-to-face, and it is me." He lowered his head and began to weep.

"It's not the same. It was self-defense. Just like my stepfather," she said as tears started to gather in her eyes.

"Tell me," Curtis pleaded, "Tell me how you felt."

"I was only thirteen. He had molested me for over five years, sneaking into my bed at night."

Curtis looked in her eyes and he understood the pain she felt.

"I had enough and decided to stop him. I gathered several weapons throughout the house and hid them in my room. I heard the familiar sound of his footsteps as he came down the hall towards my door. I laid on my bed, my hand under the pillow as I gripped the cold metal of my mother's silver candlestick."

Curtis couldn't help but feel energized as she told her story.

"It is ironic as less than a week earlier it sat on the dinner table as it held the red candle with blood-like drops that ran down its edges. Mom and Dad had received these candlesticks as a wedding present from my grandparents. They are one of the few items that Mom kept after the divorce. I saw the door handle turn slightly before I heard it. His shadow entered my room and blocked the light from the hall before he closed the door behind him. As he moved closer to my bed, I pretended to be sleeping. The smell of his cologne made me feel sick to my stomach."

Curtis didn't know what to say. Did his victims feel this way when they were abused? Did they feel like that towards him while he was trying to save them?

"I screamed, kicked him in the crotch, and grabbed the candlestick." Tears ran down her face as she raised her arm high above her head as she relived the final moments of his life. "I found him crouched on the floor writhing in pain. I looked into his eyes and said, 'You will never again hurt me or anyone else,' as I crushed the candlestick into his head."

"You harnessed the pain of five years of abuse, all the pain you suffered at his hands, the innocence that had been stolen from you. That is exactly why I do what I do," Curtis said. "I don't want anyone to suffer this pain from abuse."

"As the blood spattered onto my face, it gave me more power. I remember pieces of his brain mixed with bone and lots of blood. There was so much blood. I remember feeling proud when he was dead. I had slayed the dragon. I had won," she said as she lowered her arm still clenching the imaginary candlestick. In a whisper, she added, "I am not sure what scared me more, the monster I killed or the way I felt while I did it. I remember thinking, could I really be a killer?"

Curtis wrapped his arms around her. "You did what you had to. It is scary to see behind the mask, yours or someone else's. We will be okay. I love you!"

"I love you too!"

Curtis had moped around the homestead since they returned. They hadn't been to the Tennessee farmhouse to clean out Pappy's belongings. There was plenty of time for that. Last week was the blue moon, the second full moon in August. The past six weeks had been a whirlwind. No one fathomed that both Grandma and Pappy would be gone. Curtis had won the battle, but the personal cost was high, too high. At least Kaylee was here. If he didn't have her, he surely would have spun out of control and would never have recovered. The funeral was coming up in a couple of weeks.

It was delayed due to the publicity of his killer, The Serpent. The police were able to link him to thirty-five individual deaths, including the couple at the amusement park in Florida and Pappy. His name was Henry Blackwell, and his criminal record went all the way back to when he was an early teen. He spent his youth being passed around between foster homes, detention centers, and psychiatric facilities, and his adult life was not much different. Estranged from any immediate family, Henry was a loner and stayed in cheap apartments and long-term hotels when he wasn't in the prison system.

Curtis would never truly know how their paths crossed. Was it in Flagstaff back in the early spring? He searched his memories but could never place him. Now it didn't matter. Life moved on, and his focus now was to rebuild his life with Kaylee. He took a leave of absence from the trucking company, and Kaylee had pretty well moved in to the plantation. His life had become normal. He achieved his dream, he felt content. For the first time in his life, Curtis MacIntyre had his soulmate, and no one or nothing would take her from him.

Kaylee sat at the table. He leaned over and gave her a peck on the top of her head as he lowered himself into the chair. "You almost done writing that novel?" he joked.

"I'm just revising it now. Word count is good, I'm just polishing a few final details. Your grandfather was a remarkable man. I did not realize he was so active in local politics. His education was law, and he had been elected mayor. He has left quite the legacy. He made his mark."

A smile formed on Curtis's face as he quickly exhaled a short puff of air. "Left his mark. Pappy always said you would be judged and remembered by the mark you leave behind. I think Pappy's mark is carved deep, not only in Tennessee but within so many people. He truly transformed lives, and I know he would be honored with you writing his story."

"One of the final things Pappy said moments before the attack was that he was glad I was there and part of your lives. That acceptance means the world to me. I feel safe with you. You all have become my tribe."

"I heard him. He was whispering, but I couldn't help but overhear. He loved you. He knew you were meant to be one of us. We are linked at a higher level than we realize. Pappy believed that nothing was chance. Things happened for reasons we do not know or do not understand. People are brought together to teach each other."

"Pappy was a very wise man. We are aligned in that thinking. I, too, believe that nothing is random. Something put us together in Winslow that Saturday morning and that set a chain of events in motion that landed us here today at this very table, talking, reminiscing about this very powerful man that shaped not only our lives, but the lives of countless others. His memory will live on."

~ CHAPTER 16 ~

Two Lines, One Choice

Kaylee rushed in from her car with a pharmacy bag. She ran to the bathroom and locked the door. The box was heavy in her hand. She struggled getting it open, and her hand shook as she held the absorbent strip under the urine stream splashing on it. She and Curtis had been careful, she thought, as she once again started the timer on the counter. Three minutes. Three more minutes, and her life as she knew it would be forever altered. She would be linked to Curtis in a way that would never be severed.

What if this child inherited his desires for blood? How much was nature and how much was nurture? Could she change their child's destiny? Did she even want to have the baby? So many questions and only two minutes left until she knew for sure. Tick tock. Her sweaty hands picked up the timer and put it back down, too scared to look at the stick to see if the infamous second blue line appeared ever so slightly, getting darker and darker as the seconds ticked off the clock.

As her breathing quickened, she couldn't take it. She flipped over the stick and peered down. There was no mistake. Two dark lines stared back at her, jeered at her. Maybe it was wrong. They gave you two for a reason.

Quickly unwrapping the second test and managing to conjure up enough pee to moisten the tip of the test, she set it next to the first one and reset the timer. Three minutes. Lucky number seven. She laid the newly wetted stick in the line of pregnancy tests on the bathroom counter that taunted her as she looked at them all, showing the unmistakable result. She knew it was unlikely, but it was worth the shot. As the second line started to appear, she sank down to the cold tile floor, leaning on the massive claw-foot tub, tears streaming down her face.

She knew she couldn't tell Curtis. He would want to become a family. She loved Curtis, and they were great together, but she did not want to raise a child in his world. The last six months had been amazing. She had never felt so close to anyone before. Curtis got her. He completed her. He had given her the greatest gift anyone ever could. She had seen behind the mask, he stood before her naked, and she was not afraid. The uncontrolled shivers were not from the cold cast iron pressing against her back. She knew what she needed to do.

She grabbed a piece of paper and wrote a message to Curtis. "Mom called. I need to head to Chicago to help her with some things. I'm not sure how long I'll be. I love you more than life!" Reading it over and over in her head, she knew she needed to be gone before he got back. She couldn't face him. She needed to be strong for herself and for the baby.

She collected herself, got up, collected all the tests and wrappers scattered around the bathroom, and quickly packed a bag. She couldn't take everything as that would cause too much suspicion. She was running from a serial killer, her serial killer, but a killer nonetheless. She needed to disappear if her plan was to work.

Scrolling through her Rolodex, she came upon a name and number. She typed the number into the phone, her hand shaking as she moved the phone to her ear. She jumped as the voice on the other end answered, "Hello?"

"It's Kaylee."

"Didn't expect to hear from you. Must be something big for you to reach out."

Kaylee couldn't respond with words. The only sound on the phone was her uncontrollable sobs. "I'll transfer money. Come home," said the voice on the phone.

Kaylee finally whispered, "I'm on my way." As she lowered the phone, the line went dead.

Looking around the foyer one final time as her taxi came down the drive, she looked at her note and placed it on the table against the wall under the original artwork from *Gone with the Wind*. It was fitting, she thought as she turned and shut the massive oak door behind her.

"Kaylee?" said the voice from inside the car. "You're heading to RDU, right?"

"Yes sir, I am."

Kaylee's plane was in the air when Curtis arrived back at the house, but she wasn't on it. She couldn't leave him, not without trying. She sat at the kitchen table, her eyes red and swollen, the seven pregnancy tests lined up in front of her.

The flowers he carried dropped to the floor when he saw her.

"Kaylee, baby, what's the matter?" He dropped to his knees at her side.

"I just can't. I didn't want this. We were careful." She motioned to the line of tests laid on the table.

"A baby? We are going to have a baby?" Curtis's eyes sparked with delight as he said the words. "Kaylee, this is wonderful. We will be a family. It will be okay. Everything will be okay. You will make a wonderful mother. I love you so much!"

"I hope that love is enough, Curtis. Oh, how I hope it is!" as she lunged into his arms.

Note from the Author

I had talked about writing a fiction novel for years before finally doing it. I knew I wanted to write a suspense novel and I love romance stories, both written and film, but could I truly connect these two and weave a story? I started writing and rewriting, starting and stopping trying to follow the predefined plot I had created. As my frustration grew, I realized I just needed to let go of my preconceived notions and write the story that my heart wanted to tell. From that, *Down the Road* was born. It is a compilation of twists and turns, set in some of my favorite places, with hidden meanings sprinkled throughout. I wrote a story that I would like to read. As my first fiction novel, it was a labor of love, a learning experience, and one of my proudest accomplishments. I hope that you enjoy reading it as much as I enjoyed creating it. My hope is it inspires you to chase your dreams, as you may be surprised at how many you can catch.

Acknowledgements

I wish to acknowledge my dear friend Sara, who encouraged me one Sunday afternoon to reach for the brass ring and sign up for a writing class for fiction authors that started the ball rolling. My daughter, Casey, and husband, Tom, who supported me through countless hours of writing, hearing about my characters as they came to life, and reading scenes and drafts along the way. Without the expertise and support of Morgan Gist MacDonald and her team at Paper Raven Books, this novel would never have seen the light of day. To my editor and writing coach, Jennifer Crosswhite, Tandem Services, you have taught, encouraged, and guided me to become a true fiction author. I would also like to thank my fellow writers, my writing Pod, and countless friends and family that have offered advice, supported, and motivated me throughout this journey. Now go check something off your bucket list as I keep working on books 2 and 3 of the Driven to Kill series!

Here's a seek peek of

THE ROAD TO NOWHERE

~ CHAPTER 1 ~

Happy Family

Curtis stirred from his sound slumber by the gagging sound that came from the master bathroom. "Are you okay, Kaylee? Do you need me to get you anything?"

"No, just give me a minute," came the voice punctuated with retches and heaves and the pungent aroma that wafted into the bedroom.

He buried his head under the blankets in a futile attempt to avoid the odor and sounds coming from the mother of his unborn child. "I love you, Kaylee. I'll run down to the kitchen and get you some crackers and ginger ale."

Curtis jumped out of bed and exited the room for the safety of the lower level. He bounded down the stairs towards the kitchen, overjoyed at the reality that he finally had the family he always dreamed of. He'd lost his parents as a teen and his grandparents in the last year, but he'd found Kaylee. The love of his life. His soulmate. And now there would be a child to complete their family unit.

Curtis hummed as he grabbed the bag of saltine crackers from the pantry and poured a glass of ginger ale to take to his love. He hoped this offering to the pregnancy gods would bring some refuge and the morning sickness would be short lived.

As he walked back into the bedroom, Kaylee appeared in the doorway, her face pale, blotting her mouth with the white towel as her hair fell in clumped strands around her face.

"You got a little something in your hair?" Curtis cautiously said with a slight shake in his voice.

"Damn!" She wiped her hair with the towel. "This puking better stop soon. I can't take this. I'm going to have to cut my hair off!"

"Oh no, babe, you don't need to do that. We will figure out something. I can hold your hair as you puke," Curtis offered. A smile crept across his face as he realized how crazy that sounded.

Kaylee lowered the towel and looked up through her lashes towards Curtis as she shook her head. "You know, you never cease to amaze me."

"I'm so excited to be able to see our little baby's face today, albeit on an ultrasound screen," Kaylee mused as she buckled the seat belt over her ever-growing belly as she thought of the precious cargo growing inside. "I remember when we first heard her heartbeat just a few months ago."

"Yes!" Curtis exclaimed as he maneuvered the car down the driveway. "And hopefully we will find out if she is really a girl. I know you think she is, but you never know. Maybe we are having a son."

"I know it's a girl, Curtis," Kaylee stated matter-of-factly. "But we can wait for the doctor to confirm it."

As they pulled into the parking lot of the doctor's office, Curtis wiped the sweat from his forehead. His hand trembled as he gathered his things and they got out of the car. He took Kaylee's hand.

She looked down as she felt the cold sweat on his palm as their fingers intertwined. "Everything will be fine, Curtis. Our baby will be perfect, don't worry."

Smiling down at her, Curtis gave her hand a squeeze. "I hope so."

Kaylee struggled with the impact he might have on their child. How would the child of a serial killer look? Would there be some sign of the monster that they might become? Would a male child be more at risk than a female one?

Curtis knew she killed her abuser, but that wasn't the same. Since their paths had crossed in Winslow, Arizona, almost two years ago, this man had turned her world upside down. She would have to come clean to him soon, but not today. Today was about seeing their baby for the first time.

"Kaylee?" the nurse called as the door to the patient exam rooms opened.

"Yes." Kaylee got up from the chair in the waiting room. Instinctively, she reached for Curtis's hand. This time it was warm, soft, and strong. As she rubbed her thumb over his fingers, they headed towards the nurse waiting at the door.

"We will be in room 220," the nurse said as they headed down the hall.

Curtis shook his head.

Kaylee remembered the connection to that number. It was the time he found his mother dead. Why did it haunt him so? Why would the Universe never let him forget? She pushed the thoughts aside and focused on the excitement in the moment.

A few moments later, Kaylee laid stretched out on the exam table of the darkened ultrasound room. Both of their eyes focused on the small screen with the blinking light. As the nurse expertly navigated the wand around on Kaylee's belly, she pointed out specific measurements she was required to take. "The femur, the head, the numbers of swallows the baby makes. Is this your first child?" she asked as they hung on to every word.

"Yes, it is," Kaylee responded.

"Do you want to know what the sex is?" the nurse asked.

"Absolutely!" Curtis moved to the edge of his seat, almost falling out.

"Well, let's see if they will cooperate." She moved the wand around and snapped a few more pictures. "It's not a hundred percent, but it looks like you are having a beautiful little girl."

Kaylee and Curtis both let out a big sigh. "I knew she was a girl, Curtis!" Kaylee said confidently. "Our little princess Stephanie, we love you already." She rubbed the top of her baby bump.

As they walked through the parking lot hand in hand, the glow of meeting Stephanie lingered on their faces. "I am so excited to meet our little girl." Curtis softly stroked Kaylee's back. "Family is so important, and I am so thankful that you have given me this gift."

Kaylee shuddered at the thought of expanding their family. What would this mean? Curtis had lost his parents, his grandparents, and she didn't want to be the reason he lost his daughter, but what if? The unknown troubled her. Could Kaylee save him? Could their love overcome his monster within? What about the monster within her? Time would tell, but could she spare the time? The thoughts of doubt raced through her head.

"A penny for your thoughts?" Curtis broke through her distraction.

"Oh, Curtis, I'm sorry. I guess I am just feeling a little overwhelmed. This is all so much." She tried to convince herself as much as him as she flipped through the ultrasound pictures the nurse had printed. As she ran her finger over the profile of their daughter's face, her thoughts drifted back to that night in the park with Pappy.

As Kaylee had extended her hand to help Pappy climb over the rocks, he had whispered, *Kaylee, I'm glad Curtis found you. He is very lucky, we both are. You are good for each other. I see a future for you two, and for that I am glad. We are very blessed.* The words rang loud in her head. She stroked her hand where his lips had gently kissed her. That was one of the last memories she had of Pappy before the fight that changed their path. No one saw that coming.

Curtis glanced over at her as they drove home in silence. Her mouth was pursed, her brow furrowed, her eyes lowered as she stared at the outline of their baby's face. Her hand trembled as she studied it and traced it with her finger.

Kaylee knew the innocence of this child had them both confused. They would need to work together to protect her, to save her from the evils in the world. They needed to create a safe home for her. The plantation house at the farm would be that. In the same place that Curtis had grown up, so would Stephanie. His mother had made it warm and welcoming, and she knew that she and Curtis would carry that forward for Princess Stephanie as well. She had seen the vision in her dreams.

He reached over and placed his hand supportively on Kaylee's thigh. She twitched. His hand provided warmth;

energy moved between them, and she knew that Curtis loved her and their baby and that he would provide for them. That she did not worry about. He had money and a grand home. She had concerns about the emotional support, about the things she saw in her dreams. "We will be okay, right?" She finally broke the silence.

"I think so." His voice was quiet but shaky. "We have never done this before. Neither of us. Let's face it, neither of us really had a model childhood. I do know this; we love each other and we love this baby girl."

As her finger continued to trace the baby's profile, she said, "She has Pappy's nose."

"I think she will have a little bit of Pappy, Grandma, and Mom."

"Curtis." She paused as she lowered the picture and turned towards him. "Do you think we will be able to protect her?"

"We took down a raging lunatic serial killer in the desert; I think we can handle whatever is thrown at us, babe."

Kaylee laughed at the irony of that statement. "That's what I'm afraid of, Curtis. Do we even know what it is like to nurture and raise a person? A person that is one hundred percent reliant on us for everything. Do we have the skills to be able to instill the right values, morals? As you pointed out, neither of us have a proven track record in this area."

"You got me there. But we have four months to figure it out. Sometimes I really wish Mom and Pappy were still here. They would be a great help right now."

"We haven't killed Tucker, so we must be doing something right," Kaylee joked to lighten the mood. "But I'm not sure if you can translate taking care of Pappy's dog to taking care of a child."

"Ole Tuck is a little high maintenance for a hound, you know. So maybe there are some parallels." Curtis reached over and took her hand as they drove back to the plantation.

Tucker climbed off the wicker couch on the front porch. His tailed wagged as he stretched before he bounded down the steps to greet them. Tucker had adjusted well to life with Curtis and Kaylee after Pappy died. He still preferred to wait on the front porch for them to return home, and he developed his daily rounds where he surveyed the farm as well as the house several times a day. One of the highlights of his day involved greeting the mailman. As soon as the sound of the mail truck reached his ears, he would let out a loud welcoming howl and trot down the drive as he wagged his tail.

As Curtis and Kaylee pulled up in the Mustang, Tucker let out his welcoming howl. Tucker met them in the driveway and Curtis patted him on the head as he got out of the car.

In the darkness, Kaylee stirred. The pains were getting stronger, closer together. Her due date was still a few weeks away, but the doctor said she may come early. She clenched her jaw as the contraction ripped through her womb. As she held her breath, fists clenched, she started to tremble.

Curtis rolled over and propped himself up on one elbow. "They are getting stronger." He reached for his watch to time the contractions. "That one was over a minute, and they are almost five minutes apart."

"I think we should call the doctor. Stephanie wants to come out."

Curtis picked up the phone and dialed the number on the pad beside the bed. He spoke to the nurse and then hung up.

Kaylee looked at him as another wave of contractions ripped through her abdomen.

"They said the doctor will be calling us in a few minutes and to just keep track of the contractions." He jotted down the time and duration of the contractions on the pad of paper.

The phone rang a few minutes later. "Hello?" Curtis answered. "Kaylee, Dr. Silver wants to talk to you." He handed the phone to her.

Kaylee fought to catch her breath after the last contraction. "They are getting stronger." The reality of becoming a parent started to sink in. In a short time, she and Curtis would meet Princess Stephanie. Would Stephanie have her green eyes? Would she have strong hands like her dad, or long delicate fingers like her mom?

Dr. Silver's voice on the other end of the phone jolted her back into the present. "Kaylee? Kaylee? Are you okay? Are you still there?"

"Yes, yes, I am still here. What did you ask?"

"Come to the hospital. I am already here, so I'll see you as soon as you get settled in your room."

Curtis was already out of bed and heading to the bathroom. They had planned this out. The bags were packed and by the door ready for Curtis to put them in the Mustang's trunk. When he came out of the bathroom, Kaylee was sitting on the edge of the bed. "Are you okay? Can you get up?"

"Just give me a second." She pushed herself off the bed, and Curtis helped her stand.

"Let's get you downstairs." He guided her towards the door.

As they reached the bottom of the stairs, another contraction hit. Kaylee bent over and moaned as the pain shot through her. «My back!" she screamed.

Curtis rubbed her lower back as they showed him during the birthing classes. It didn't seem to help, as Kaylee continued to moan as the contraction intensified.

After several minutes, she straightened up.

"That was a long one. We better get going or Stephanie is going to be a home birth."

Kaylee smiled as he helped her to the car.

Curtis ran back and grabbed the suitcases and hurled them into the trunk. The Mustang's engine roared to life as he turned the key and they headed down the drive.

Kaylee couldn't help but glance in the back seat to make sure the car seat was in place. Curtis had installed it the week before. *Car seat, check.*

Her dream was more vivid last night. It became clearer and clearer as the delivery day drew closer. She saw the death that followed Curtis. She struggled the last four months with when to tell Curtis. Now was not the time, not today.